seaside

G·K
Hall
&Co.

Also by Terri Blackstock
in Large Print:

Evidence of Mercy
Justifiable Means
Ulterior Motives
Presumption of Guilt
Never Again Good-bye
When Dreams Cross
Blind Trust
Broken Wings

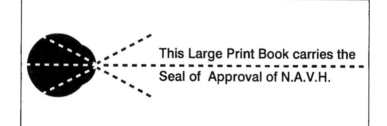

Terri Blackstock

seaside

G.K. Hall & Co. • **Waterville, Maine**

Published in 2001 by arrangement with
Zondervan Publishing House.

G.K. Hall Large Print Inspirational Series.

The text of this Large Print edition is unabridged.
Other aspects of the book may vary from the original edition.

Set in 16 pt. Plantin by Al Chase.

Printed in the United States on permanent paper.

Library of Congress Cataloging-in-Publication Data

Blackstock, Terri, 1957–
    Seaside : a novella / Terri Blackstock.
        p.   cm.
    ISBN: 0-7838-9511-9 (lg. print : hc : alk. paper)
    1. Mothers and daughters — Fiction.   2. Women photographers
— Fiction.   3. Seaside resorts — Fiction.   4. Beaches — Fiction.
5. Sisters — Fiction.   6. Florida — Fiction.   7. Large type books.
I. Title.
PS3552.L34285 S43 2001b
    813'.54—dc 21   2001024920

This book is lovingly dedicated to the Nazarene

chapter one

Maggie Downing didn't like endings or beginnings. She preferred to keep things somewhere in the middle, where she could build her momentum — no jolting starts or screeching halts. Momentum was critical, she'd always told her daughters. Useful people didn't veer off course, and they never slowed at the hurdles.

But she had been wrong.

Why had it taken her fifty-five years to learn it?

She sat on the deck of her split-level condo, looking out at the faint, foggy outline of the Rockies. She had photographed them many times, and collected the prints in a book that adorned thousands of coffee tables now. The Tourist Bureau of Colorado used one of her pictures for their advertisements, complete with her signature in the corner. But that was just one of the many successes she'd had. She had the gift of turning beauty into bucks, a friend had once facetiously told her. Nothing was wasted.

The brisk wind made her shiver, and she pulled her sweater tighter. She longed for the warm air, the smell of salt on the wind, the sound of foamy waves whooshing onto the sand. She had moved to Colorado to escape the heat and humidity of the South, but by March, she was always weary of winter.

She knew her girls were weary, too, in their own corners of the world. But their fatigue had little to do with the cold.

She thought she heard the phone ringing, so she sprang up and went in. By the time she reached it, she realized that she had only imagined it. Probably, neither Sarah nor Corinne had gotten her messages yet. She had left one message with an unreliable machine, and the other with a less reliable grandchild. She hoped they would call back.

The Tiffany lamp across the little parlor cast a warm glow on the antique table on which it sat. She needed to pack away the pictures and memorabilia she had spread across it. Sarah and Corinne could help her decide what to do with all of them. The two girls might even enjoy seeing the pictures of themselves frozen in time, laughing and crying and staring and dancing and growing over the years. She had documented all of the awards, all the accolades, all the accomplishments . . .

All the usefulness.

She wished just once she had spent quiet time with them, walking along abandoned beaches, sailing on quiet waters, fishing on a lonely pier. If she had her child-rearing to do over, she would take them outside at night and lie on a blanket, staring at the stars. She would teach them to breathe the breeze that caressed their faces, to savor the scent of jasmine, to walk for pleasure and not for exercise.

But, until lately, those joys had somehow escaped her. Life had been a series of ventures, one deadline piled upon another. She had rushed through her life, building her momentum and chalking up her feats, and had taught her daughters to do the same.

She picked the phone back up; listened to make sure it had a dial tone. They would call back soon. Any minute now, one of them would get home and return her call.

She went into the kitchen. The scent of vanilla and cinnamon lingered from the rolls she'd baked for a friend yesterday. She had never baked much before, and had found in the last few weeks that it was one of those slow, simple pleasures she'd neglected in the past. She planned to do a lot more of it.

She walked to the coffeepot, an archaic percolator, and filled it with coffee grounds. She added the water and set it to brew, then took the water pot from her windowsill and began to water the ferns spilling over their hanging baskets.

As she did, she practiced the speech she had prepared for Sarah and Corinne. She had to be persuasive without being overbearing. Talking them into dropping everything and spending a week with her in Florida was not going to be easy. She had taught them well. Sarah's husband and two children had not shaken her free of the lessons Maggie had so carefully programmed into her. And Corinne's three businesses were testimony that the family way worked.

When the coffee finished brewing, she poured a cup and went back into the little parlor, accented with antiques and eclectic art pieces she'd picked up in her travels. Her hard work had bought her each valuable piece, from the polished secretary against the wall to the acrylic resin sculpture on a pedestal in the corner. But things held little meaning for her now.

She wanted to be with her daughters. The three of them needed a time for mending fences, for healing relationships, for explanations and exhortations.

She picked up the phone and called the airline. She would buy their tickets, and perhaps that would force their hands. She was willing to do whatever it took to get them there.

She hoped it wasn't too late to show them that time wasted is not always a waste of time.

chapter two

Corinne Downing sat at a red light holding the cell phone to her ear, growing more and more irritated. Wasn't it just like her sister to put her on hold for so long when Sarah knew she was on a cell phone in her car? That was the story of her life. Just put Corinne on hold. Let time tick by, minutes, hours, years at a time, while everyone else's life moved on.

Sarah clicked back on. "Sorry about that. It was the intercession speaker for the prayer conference next week. She canceled, so now I'm stuck finding another one. Now, where were we? Oh, yes. Mom."

"She really wants us to go, Sarah. It's all about this autobiography she's doing. She wants pictures of us together — like I really want my picture stamped on the cover of ten thousand books. I don't know what's gotten into her. This has become so important, she'll do just about anything. And she's already bought our airline tickets. How's that for confidence?"

"She *what?*" Sarah asked.

"She thinks if she has the tickets, we have to go. She just won't take no for an answer."

"Well, we're grown women, Corinne," Sarah

said. "She'll *have* to take no for an answer."

"But then there's that 'Honor your mother' thing," Corinne said. "Part of me keeps thinking that I'd better do what she says."

"Or what?" Sarah asked. "Is she going to ground you? For heaven's sake, you're twenty-eight years old. I'm thirty-three. I don't have time for this." The phone beeped again, and she moaned. "Hold on, Corinne."

Corinne was certain her blood pressure climbed as she waited. She reached her tiny duplex with its termites and peeling paint, and pulled into the driveway, still holding the phone to her ear. As she got out of the car, she looked down at the spot on her jeans. What had she been thinking, adding a dog-walking business to her other struggling enterprises? Designing Web sites kept her swamped enough, and her jewelry business filled most of her free time.

And now look at her. An overzealous cocker spaniel had urinated on her today. She had about two hours before she needed to walk the dogs again — not nearly enough time to go in and work on the Web site that had cratered yesterday. If she didn't get it done today, she would lose the client for sure. And then she wouldn't be able to pay her car note this month, and they'd repossess it, and she'd have to go to her mother for a loan, admitting that she couldn't make ends meet . . .

Yet here she was, on her cell phone — *long distance* — waiting for her sister to come back to the phone. She went into the house and slammed the door, as if Sarah could hear.

As if on cue, her sister clicked back on. "Corinne, you still there?"

"Of course I'm still here," she snapped, "but I'm on a cell phone and these calls are expensive. I didn't call you to be put on hold. You're not some major corporation with automated phone lines, you know."

"Well, excuse me," Sarah said. "I have things going on, and I have people living in this house besides me."

"Look, just forget I called," Corinne spouted. "I thought you'd like to know that Mom bought the airline tickets. That's all I wanted to tell you."

"Fine," Sarah said. "Thanks for the info." With that, the phone went dead.

Corinne clicked the "off" button and threw her cell phone onto the faded, threadbare couch she had salvaged when a friend had replaced his. The phone bounced and fell to the floor. She let out a yell of pure frustration, then turned her computer on. Shuffling papers around on the rickety table that served as her desk, she told herself there was no way she was going to spend a week *anywhere* with her sister. And her mother was better off for it, whether she realized it or not.

chapter three

Sarah slammed the phone back into its cradle. "I don't believe her! She's just like my mother!"

"What did *she* do, offer you a week in Hawaii?"

Her husband's sarcasm stung. She wheeled around and watched him as he kicked off his tennis shoes, green from just-cut grass. "Tell me what you want me to do, Jim! Do you want me to drop everything, pack a bag, and head off to Florida without you and the kids for a week? Is that it? Because I don't think you have the slightest inkling of what I do around here while you're in the courtroom playing Matlock."

She went to the medicine cabinet and pulled out a bottle of Tylenol.

"Look at you," he said, following her barefoot across the carpet. "Your head hurts and your stomach is probably in knots."

"Well, what do you expect? I have a mother who wants me to drop everything and fly off to Florida for a week, a sister with a chip on her shoulder the size of Mount Saint Helens, and a husband who has the gall to be sarcastic at a time like this." She poured out two caplets and washed them down. Turning back to Jim, she tried to calm herself. "I have responsibilities,

Jim. I'd love to take off for a week, but I can't."

"Why not?" he asked. "If my parents offered me an all-expenses-paid week in Florida, I'd jump on it. Most husbands would have a problem with it, but I'm giving you my blessing. I think you *need* a vacation."

"Every mother needs a vacation," she said, dropping into the easy chair she rarely sat in. "But it's not realistic. What kind of mother would I be if I did that? What kind of wife? What kind of conference chairman?"

"What kind of daughter will you be if you say no to your mother? It's obviously important to her."

"So I choose my guilt?" She hated it when he made things sound so easy. He didn't have a clue. "When you go out of town, you pack your bag, get on the plane, and go. When *I* go, I have to cook enough meals for a week, make sure everyone has enough clean clothes, lay out what Jenny and Chase will wear to school every day, make sure they can go home with friends in the afternoons, arrange for rides to the zillion things they have to do every day —"

As she spoke, he breathed an annoyed laugh, shook his head, and moved to the sink. He turned the faucet on full blast and began to wash his hands. Her words drowned in the noise.

She got up, seething, and watched him grab the hand towel she'd hung there this morning. He always did that when she made him mad — turned up the television or the car radio or created some other racket that covered her words.

"Why do you do that?" she asked. "Just cut me off like that?"

As if it took great effort, he turned the water off and looked at her in the mirror. "Because you're exaggerating, Sarah, and it's a little demeaning. When I travel, I know you're at home taking care of things. So I don't have to make a million arrangements — you've got things under control. But you could do the same thing when you travel. *I'm* here. I may not do things exactly the way you would, but I'm not an incompetent imbecile either. I can feed the kids, they can dress themselves, and I can get them where they need to be."

"It's not just the kids!" she said, her voice rising again. "I'm right in the middle of planning a prayer conference, I have that dinner for your office that we're hosting in this very house, the literacy program is just getting off the ground, and I'm in charge —"

"You can postpone a couple of deadlines or get other people to fill in. Call a caterer to handle the dinner party. It's not for two more weeks. And just tell them you can't attend the prayer conference. You're great at delegating, Sarah."

She wondered if he could really be that dense. "Do you hear yourself? Do you know how hard it is to get people to volunteer for things? That's why *I* do everything! And if I leave the kids' schedules to you, you'll just blow them off because you hate to rush and you don't think any of

16

it is all that important."

He slapped the towel down. "What is the worst thing that could happen, Sarah, if Jenny missed a dance lesson? If Chase missed one soccer practice?"

"See there?" she threw back at him. "I *can't* count on you. You're already rationalizing not getting them there."

The color on his face had nothing to do with the work he'd just done in the yard. "Go to Florida, Sarah," he said, matching her volume. "Your mother wants you to go. *I* want you to go."

She hadn't expected it, and it knocked the wind out of her. Was her marriage on the rocks? Had she been too busy to notice it?

Time froze, and her heart raced. Their angry eyes locked. He didn't appreciate her. He deserved to have to fill her shoes for a week. He deserved to have to cook whatever he ate, and spend hours a day in the car, and dig through the laundry for underwear. He deserved to miss her.

Wearily, she wondered if he would.

The phone shrilled, and seconds later the bedroom door burst open. "Mom, it's for you!" their ten-year-old daughter shouted. "Grandma again."

"I'm coming, Jenny," she said.

"Mom, can Eric Holmes spend the night?" Their eight-year-old stumbled in, covered with mud from his knees to the bottoms of his sneakers. She knew he had tracked it all the

17

way through the house.

"I don't know right now," she said weakly. "Chase, you're tracking mud . . ."

"Oops!" he cried, noticing it for the first time. "I'm going. But can he, Mom? I need an answer right now."

"Then no."

"But his mom is out of town and he'll have to stay by himself."

She almost bought it, but she knew Eric's mother. "I don't think so, Chase. He's eight years old. She would never leave him alone. Nice try, though."

The boy slunk from the room, and Sarah turned back to her husband. Had he really told her he wanted her to go? The words still stung.

"Why are you so mad at me?" she asked in a quieter voice.

"I'm not mad," he said, lowering his as well. "Don't change the subject. This is about your schedule and your mother's invitation."

"It was not an invitation. It was a demand."

"Well, you're good at meeting demands. It's what you do."

She didn't think he meant that as a compliment. "Last time I looked, you were making demands right along with everyone else. And now you want a break from me?"

His dull eyes confirmed it. "Tell you what, Sarah. Either you go with your mother to Florida for a week, or I will. But it would be good for one of us to get out of here for a while."

18

"Fine," she clipped. She crossed the bedroom and picked up the cordless phone lying on the table. "I'll go. My mother wins, and you win. Everybody else loses."

Jim didn't respond. She clicked on the phone and brought it to her ear. By the time she turned around, he was gone.

chapter four

When Corinne got the message that Sarah had changed her mind, she sat quietly in her computer chair, her arms around her knees, her head tucked between them. She couldn't believe it. Sarah had been so adamant about not going just hours ago, and now she had done a 180. What had gotten into her? Corinne couldn't imagine.

It had been easy to turn the invitation down when she knew her sister wasn't going. But now the whole thing would eat at her if she *didn't* go. She would spend the week wondering how her mother and sister were bonding, if they were talking about her, if they were trying to work out her future for her, and if they were pitying her for the things she didn't have.

No, she couldn't let that happen. She had to go, even if it was inconvenient. She looked up at her computer screen, bewildered at the Web site she hadn't been able to fix. She couldn't afford to lose this client. Maybe she could take her laptop with her and figure out the problem on the plane. She could handle her calls from Florida. She'd have to find someone else to walk her dog clients, and she could postpone the two jewelry parties she'd scheduled. The money she'd lose would hurt, but maybe she could juggle her credit cards for one more month.

With no choice but to react as expected, she picked up the telephone and called her mother to tell her she would come.

chapter five

Maggie got to Florida a day early to prepare the cabin her friend Milton had found for her. He was waiting for her there, and held his arms open as she got out of the rental car.

"Milton! Look at you," she said, walking into his hug. "You never age, for heaven's sake."

"Tell that to my joints," he said with a smile. "You look great, Mags. God's still favoring you, isn't he?"

She laughed. "He's had his work cut out for him lately."

He took her bag out of the trunk, and with his other arm around her, escorted her up the steps to the cabin.

She had met Milton — twenty years her senior — at a photography conference a decade ago, and they had bonded when she'd helped him get his first book of prints published. They had become close friends over the years, and talked on the phone often. Several times a year, they met at conferences and spent time together. He still made a living as a portrait photographer, but he had done quite well with his book, and she had great admiration for his sensitive artist's eye and his vulnerable heart.

Many times, she had been grateful for the blessing of their friendship. When she couldn't share a crisis with her family, it was good to have a godly friend who could help carry the burden and remind her that the Lord was still in control.

But there were too many miles between them. It had been his idea for her to come to Florida for a week, and at her request he had found this cabin in a quiet, as-yet-undiscovered part of the beach.

He opened the cabin door and led her inside. She caught her breath at the sight of the ocean view from the picture window. The glass doors were open, and the warm salty breeze greeted her. She closed her eyes and savored the peace. "Oh, Milton. You did good."

"I hope you like it. It's called Seaside."

She stepped out onto the deck, squinting in the sunlight. She couldn't see anyone in either direction. Sea gulls squawked out over the water, and the waves frothed as they rolled against the shore. "The girls won't believe it," she whispered.

Milton came out and leaned against the rail, looking at her. "I've been praying for you, Mags. I hope the week is everything you want it to be."

She nodded. "It won't be easy."

He pushed off from the rail, and she saw the slump in his back as he turned, leaned over it, and looked out. "If you get that perfect shot you're looking for, you can use my darkroom. It's just a few miles into town. You remember how to get there, don't you?"

"I can find it," she said. She reached up and pressed a kiss on her old friend's weathered face. He slid his arms around her again, and held her tight for a moment. It felt like family — like a brother whose comforting arms made everything all right. The two of them had never been an item. He had been deliriously in love with his wife, and had never quite gotten over her sudden death three years ago. Maggie had helped him through that.

They had seen each other through a lot.

"Well," he said, breaking the hug and checking his watch. "I have an appointment at three, so I'd better get back. I have to take a portrait of three toddlers. I hope they've had their naps." He kissed her forehead and started into the house. "I know you need to be alone for a while, anyway. Call me if you need me, Mags. I'm not far away."

As she heard his car pulling out of the parking lot behind the cabin, she gazed out at the majesty of the Gulf, testimony to the sovereignty of a God who held her in the palm of his scarred hand. She knew he would take care of the week.

chapter six

The next day, Maggie was waiting at Corinne's gate when she got off the plane. She had never been so glad to see her younger daughter. She almost knocked a man down trying to get to her.

She could see from the way Corinne looked right through her at first that her daughter almost hadn't recognized her. Maggie wasn't surprised; she knew she had changed a lot in the last year.

"Mom?"

Maggie threw her arms around Corinne and embraced her as if she'd come back from the dead. "I'm so glad you came, Corinne."

Corinne seemed unused to displays of affection. Maggie hoped someone in her daughter's life was hugging her on a regular basis.

"Mom, you've lost weight. And your hair —"

"You like it short?" Maggie asked. "I don't even have to blow-dry it." She grabbed one of Corinne's bags. "Sarah's not here yet. Her flight was delayed."

She glanced back and saw the tension Corinne always got when Sarah's name was mentioned. "Of course it was."

"Now what does that mean?"

Corinne sighed. "For most of my life, I've waited for Sarah. At nearly every family function, every dinner, every event, Sarah's been late. Why should this be different?"

"It's not as if she did this on purpose," Maggie said, raising her voice to be heard over the crowd hurrying toward the baggage claim. She was glad Corinne just had a carry-on.

"I know," Corinne said. "It's just so typical. It's not her fault. It just *seems* like it's her fault."

"Well, we might as well make the most of it," Maggie said. "She was delayed an hour and a half, so let's just go find a place to sit and get a cup of coffee. Maybe we could have a little pie."

Corinne grinned and looked askance at her mother. "You? Mom, you didn't lose all that weight by eating pie."

"I'm on vacation," Maggie declared. "I don't diet when I'm on vacation. In fact, I may never diet again. Getting skinny has taught me one thing. Skinny people look old faster. I've decided to put a little weight back on my bones to smooth out the wrinkles."

"I can't do that," Corinne said, "because young people look better skinny. Truth is, I'd like to find a place where I can plug in my laptop and get a little work done. I need to hook up my modem so I can check my e-mail. If we're just going to be sitting idle for an hour and a half, I might as well get something done."

Maggie's heart sank. Yes, she had taught her daughter well. She tried not to let her disappointment show. "Well, you could sit and talk to your mother whom you haven't seen in over a year. That wouldn't exactly be idle time."

Corinne seemed amused. "It's not that I don't want to do that, Mom. It's that we're going to have a whole week together."

"You're also going to have a whole week to plug your modem in if you need to."

"How about we compromise?" Corinne asked. "I'll check my e-mail and spend about fifteen or twenty minutes on it at most, and then we go have a cup of coffee and a piece of pie."

Maggie could see the fatigue and anxiety on Corinne's face. Maybe if she took care of things now, she wouldn't worry about them later. "All right," Maggie said.

They found a row of telephone booths with modem hookups. Several people sat pounding on their laptops with focused urgency. Corinne hurried over and plugged in. "I'll just be a minute, Mom."

"I'm going to duck into this newsstand and buy a magazine," Maggie said. "I'll be back in a few minutes."

Maggie bought a magazine and a cup of coffee, then came back and sat on a padded bench not far from her daughter. She had pictured Corinne and herself laughing and talking, catching up, as they waited for Sarah's plane. She wanted to know more about her younger daughter's life than she got from weekly telephone tag and hurried exchanges, but Corinne was banging on that computer as if the fate of the world depended on whatever she was typing. Now and then she would pick up the phone, dial a number, and talk animatedly, all the while punching on the keyboard. She supposed she should be proud of her enterprising daughter.

She reached into her camera bag and pulled out her camera, snapped on the lens she wanted, held it up, and focused it. She took a picture of Corinne holding the phone between her shoulder and ear as she punched on the keyboard, her eyes drilling into the screen. It was the quintessential picture of Corinne, Maggie thought. All work and no play. She supposed she had come by it honestly.

She put the camera up and flipped through the magazine. By the time she finished it, an hour and fifteen minutes had passed. Corinne looked no closer to stopping than she had when she'd started. Sighing heavily, Maggie picked her things back up and walked over to her daughter. "Corinne, we need to get to the gate. Sarah's plane will be here in fifteen minutes."

Corinne looked up at her as if she'd forgotten she was there. "Oh, Mom, I'm sorry. I said we'd have that pie, didn't I? And you wanted coffee."

"Don't worry about it. I got some."

"Oh, good." She shook her head and started trying to close the computer down. "This is a nightmare, Mom. I designed this Web site and I can't figure out what's wrong with it. They're losing sales because customers are getting hung up placing their orders. If I lose this client, I'm going to lose a major part of my income. And I don't know if I could replace them, at least not with one client."

"I understand," Maggie said, trying not to look like a martyr.

"I mean, that's the only reason I was so resistant to coming on this trip. I knew that I was going to have to take care of this." She snapped the computer shut, put it back in her briefcase, and gathered her things. Maggie took Corinne's suitcase and rolled it behind her. "But I promise I won't be doing this all week," Corinne continued. "Only what's absolutely necessary."

But as they walked back through the concourse, Maggie knew that the two of them had radically different ideas about what was necessary.

Sarah tried not to let the surprise show on her face when she got off the plane and saw her mother and Corinne standing at the end of the ramp waiting for her. Her mother hadn't told her that she had cut her hair so short, or that she had lost so much weight. Sarah wondered if she had been eating right. There had been many times, while Sarah and Corinne were growing up, when their mother had been so busy she had forgotten to eat. Maybe this new book was affecting her that way; maybe she wasn't taking care of herself.

Her mother drew Sarah into a hug as soon as she reached her, but Corinne hung back with that usual strained look on her face. "We thought you'd never get here," Corinne said, giving her a noncommittal hug when Maggie let her go.

"*I* thought I'd never get here," Sarah said. "They had us sitting out on the runway for an hour and a half before we took off. It was a nightmare. A total waste of time." She started to walk, pulling her carry-on suitcase behind her. Her mother and sister fell in beside her.

"I think a nightmare would be more like the engine catching fire, the landing gear not going down," Corinne told her.

"That's right," Maggie said. "Sitting out on the runway for an hour and a half could be a blessing to some people."

"Yeah, I know," Sarah said. "The lady next to me read the whole time. She didn't finish her book, and she was almost disappointed when we started to land. But I've got better things to do than sit still for an hour and a half." She glanced at her sister. "So how was your flight?"

"Fast, uneventful," Corinne clipped. Corinne looked pretty, as she always did. Her hair was flawless, and she wore just enough makeup to accent her still youthful features. *She must wear a size four,* Sarah thought with a rush of envy. Corinne always had been small. Sarah felt like a walrus in comparison.

"So, Mom, what made you cut your hair?"

Her mother's smile faded slightly. "You don't like it, do you?"

"Sure I like it," Sarah said. "But you always said that real women had long hair."

"And since when did you ever listen to anything I said?" She chuckled and shook her head. "I just got tired of messing with it. You should try it," she said. "In the mornings after I get out of the shower I towel-dry it, and I don't have to do anything else to it. I should have done it years ago."

"We've got to hook you up with some better earrings," Corinne piped in. "Something a little more colorful around your face. Maybe I brought a few things you could use."

"That's my sister," Sarah said. "Always trying to make a sale."

Corinne shot her a look. "I'm not trying to make a sale. I'll give them to her if she wants them."

Aware that she was dangerously close to offending her sister — which was not difficult to do — Sarah changed the subject and pulled out snapshots of her kids.

∂∞

They drove for an hour and a half in the car Maggie had rented, the Gulf in clear view for the last half hour. "Remember the last time we were here?" Sarah asked.

Corinne smiled. "I think that was the last family vacation we took. I must have been five."

31

"And Sarah was ten," Maggie said. "We planned it for months, then got hit with a hurricane. It rained every single day. You girls fought the whole time." She shook her head. "I swore never to do it again." Her gaze drifted to the blue, whitecapped waves pounding against the shore. "That was a mistake," she said in a softer voice. "We should have tried again."

They passed the hotels, and the beach houses gradually got farther and farther apart. Maggie finally pulled into the driveway of one situated alone on a quiet patch of beach. She enjoyed the oohs and aahs that marked the girls' approval. "The cabin is named Seaside."

"Wow, Mom. This is great!" Corinne said as they got out of the car. "Listen. You can hear the waves from right here."

"There's a beautiful view from the cabin," Maggie said. "The whole back wall is glass. You can open the glass doors at night and listen to the waves. It's very private."

Sarah gave her mother a bewildered look. "What's gotten into you, spending so much money? You're the one who used to want to stay in the cheapest place we could find and bring our own groceries."

"Well, I did buy a few groceries," Maggie said. "We're going to eat out a lot, but tonight I wanted to cook out on the grill and eat on the deck. It's just so beautiful, and it's nice and cool out. Not muggy like it is in the summer."

Sarah and Corinne shot each other a look that

said this was totally out of character. Maggie smiled. She hoped it *was* out of character, because she wanted this week to be a new beginning, something that would mark a change in their lives. She owed it to them.

But more than that, she owed it to herself. These were her girls, after all. Her own flesh and blood. Much of what they knew and how they functioned came from her teaching. And now she wanted to teach them something she'd never taught them before. She wanted to teach them where to find peace.

But as they began unloading the car and taking things inside, she wondered whether either of them was in any shape to learn it.

chapter seven

Sarah had grown up with a camera in her face, recording her every move, but she wasn't in the mood for it now. If she'd had more notice, she'd have dieted. She could just imagine how the pictures her mother was taking now would look, with her face twice the size of Corinne's.

It ruined her appetite.

She got up and began clearing the dishes, just to escape that lens. "Sarah, you can't be finished," her mother protested. "You hardly ate a thing!"

"I wasn't really hungry," she said. She dumped her plate in the sink with a clatter and turned the water on. It drowned the conversation at the table, which was fine with her. Corinne was as full of sarcastic barbs as Jim was, and now she was chattering to her mother, emphasizing her point by waving around the cell phone she had just pulled out of her briefcase.

That reminded Sarah that she needed to call home and check on the kids. She wondered if her replacement for the prayer conference had remembered to pick up the programs from the printer. She wondered if Jim had driven the car pool to Jenny's cheerleading practice. And she suddenly remembered Jim's attitude the other day when *he'd* turned the water on, cutting *her* off.

She looked up; her mother's camera was pointed at her again. She cut off the water and raised a hand to cover her face. "Mom, please."

"Oh, no, you've got to be kidding me!" Corinne sprang to her feet, studying the display of her cell phone. "I can't get a signal. Mom! What am I gonna do?"

"Use the cabin telephone," Maggie shrugged.

"But people have my cell number! They have to be able to get in touch with me!"

"So call them and tell them our number."

"Mom, you don't understand!" Corinne's face blazed as if she'd been to the beach without sunscreen. "They can't know I'm out of town. V-Tech's Web site is in crisis, and if they know I picked this week to hop off on vacation —"

"No wonder the kids haven't called," Sarah said, grabbing her purse with wet hands. She pulled out her own cell phone and tried it. "Nope. No signal." She tried not to react as emotionally as her sister, though the prospect of being un-reachable disturbed her. She had promised Dana, her surrogate chairperson for the prayer confer-ence, that she could call her with any questions.

Corinne was still trying to get a signal when Sarah grabbed the phone on the wall.

"What are you doing?" Corinne asked.

Sarah dialed her calling-card number. "Calling home."

"But I was about to use the phone!"

Sarah cut her a look. "I won't be long."

Corinne plopped back down with exaggerated frustration.

Chase answered the phone. "Rivers' House of Pancakes."

Sarah frowned. "Chase?"

"Mom!"

"What's this about pancakes?"

"It was a joke, Mom," he said. "Daddy's been trying to call your cell phone. You want to talk to him?"

"Well, okay," she said. "But how are you doing? Are things going okay at home?"

"They're fine," he said.

"And how was school today?"

"Fine."

"How was your test?"

"Fine."

She wondered how the eight-year-old could go from Robin Williams to Joe Friday in a matter of seconds. "Is that all you can say to your mother?"

"Guess what we're having for supper?" he asked.

She was pretty sure this was a trick question. "What?"

"Pie!"

She felt a rush of blood to her face, certain that this was Jim's deliberate attempt to bait her.

She looked at her mother and sister, as if they'd heard everything and were judging her.

But they weren't listening. Her mother had the camera lens on Corinne now, and her sister was moving around the cabin and holding the phone in different positions, trying to get a signal.

"Let me talk to Daddy." Sarah waited a moment as Chase passed the phone to his father.

"Hey," he said. "How was your flight?"

"Fine," she clipped, turning away from Corinne and her mother and lowering her voice. "What's this about pie for supper?"

"Come on, Sarah. You're out of town. I'm in charge. I'm handling things."

"You cannot feed our kids pie for supper."

"I can feed them whatever I want."

"But I spent all afternoon Saturday making meals for you to eat. I wanted to make sure they would have balanced nutrition while I was gone."

"They're not going to wind up in the hospital because they eat sweets one night."

She glanced over her shoulder. They still weren't listening. "But you're undermining me, Jim," she said in a harsh whisper. "They're going to love being with you and hate being with me. They're going to think I'm the one that makes them walk like soldiers and you're the one who has a party when I'm gone."

"Well, is that so bad? I mean, most of the time you're the one taking care of them and I'm at work. What's wrong with me being the good guy for a change?"

"I don't want my kids' teeth to rot out before I get home."

"Your kids' teeth are not going to rot out. They're going to be just fine. Now, if you can stop obsessing for just a minute, I have to give you a message from Dana."

"Oh, no," she said. "What?"

"She said that she went to proof the new programs and they misspelled *conference* on the front."

"No way!" she cried. She had her mother's and her sister's attention now. "I saw the proofs. I would have noticed!"

"Well, the printer says it's not his fault because no one caught it in the proofs. He's going to do them over, but he's charging you again."

"*He* messed them up! I can't believe this. Why didn't you tell her not to accept that?"

"She told him to go ahead and reprint them. And you can stop yelling at me because I'm not involved in this at all. I'm just a messenger."

She pressed her temple. Her head ached again. "Look, will you call her and tell her to go back and make sure the church doesn't get charged again? We have a budget! And the new programs have got to be ready by Thursday, or they're useless. Does the printer understand that?"

Her mother came up behind her and started massaging her shoulders.

"Sarah, I don't know what he understands," Jim said. "I'm working on a case and trying to be the single parent this week. I don't have time to do your volunteer work for you."

"If you remember," she said, choosing her words carefully so her mother wouldn't read between the lines, "this was your idea."

"What was? Going to Florida?"

"Yes," she bit out.

"And it's wonderful to see how much you're relaxing," he said. "I know this is going to come as a surprise to you, but the world is not going to crumble if your programs don't get done right. One misspelled word, or even an extra bill, is not going to bring your world crashing to a halt."

The back door slid open, and Corinne went outside. Her mother abandoned Sarah's shoulders and followed her brooding daughter out. Sarah stretched the cord into the bedroom, in case they could still hear. "I can't tell you how much it means to me to know that my husband respects the work I do so much!" she whispered. "You think that nothing I do is worthwhile. And feeding my kids *junk* —"

"They're my kids, too," he cut in.

"So you have the right to poison them?"

He laughed then, but it was a dry, humorless laugh full of indictment. "You're overreacting, Sarah."

"And you're *under*reacting. You told me to come, and now I'm here, but you're treating my kids and my commitments like they don't matter a whit —"

Anger rippled in his voice. "Sarah, there are other things more important —"

"Like what? Feeding your children pie?"

39

"Yeah," he said. "Sometimes. Sometimes maybe that's just what they need to be fed. Maybe you, Corinne, and your mother need to eat pie on the beach tonight. It might help your disposition."

She grunted, and he sighed. His voice softened a little.

"Stop worrying, Sarah," he said. "I'm not treating this like a frat house party. We're doing homework, getting our baths, and I'm putting the kids to bed on time. But meanwhile, we're going to eat pie — lemon ice box — and we're going to get ice cream, and we're going to lie on the floor and watch *Old Yeller*."

It didn't sound quite so bad when he put it that way. But it was still a Mom-Is-Gone Celebration.

"So I've delivered the message," Jim said, "and I've checked on you to see if you got there all right. And now that we've exchanged these little rays of sunshine, I think I'll get back to the kids."

Sarah rushed back into the kitchen and slammed the phone in its cradle without saying good-bye. She went into the bathroom, splashed water on her face to get rid of the tears, quickly dabbed it all away, then freshened up her makeup so that there would be no evidence that she had cried. Then, trying to look bouncy, she went back out. Her mother and Corinne had walked out toward the beach. Good. That would give her a few moments to calm herself.

40

The tears came again, and she let them fall. They wouldn't help, though — wouldn't solve a single thing. But she still had to get them out of her system and straighten up before her mom and sister came back in. People in her family weren't vulnerable. They weren't soft. They weren't emotional. No, the women of her family were useful. Useful was the most important thing to be.

Even if it made her family glad that she was gone.

chapter eight

The moment Sarah got her husband on the phone, that familiar wave of contempt had washed over Corinne again. Corinne didn't want to call it jealousy. She knew other people would if they knew what she felt, but it wasn't that, really. She didn't wish misery on her sister. She just couldn't avoid the memories of Sarah excelling at everything as they grew up.

Sarah overachieved. She accomplished things. Her footsteps had always been hard to follow. She was sharp and quick and organized. If *she* had three businesses, they would all be Fortune 500. She had met her husband in college and married the month after she graduated, and here Corinne was, twenty-eight years old, and she still hadn't met the right person.

She stepped off the deck and walked across the sand. The sun was just beginning to set on the horizon, leaving an orange glow on the water. It was almost blinding, yet she walked toward it. In moments, her mother was out beside her.

"Corinne, are you okay?"

Corinne turned around and tried to plant a smile on her face. "Of course, Mom. I'm fine."

"You just looked a little sad when you walked

out here. I thought maybe that competition between you and Sarah was rearing its ugly head again."

"I'm not competing with her," she said. "We might as well be in two separate universes. They have very little to do with each other. I don't want her life, and she doesn't want mine."

"Well, now, that's a cold statement if I ever heard one," her mom said.

"Oh, come on, Mom. You think I want to be tied down to a husband and two kids? Driving my little minivan all around town, going to soccer games, dance practices, and PTA meetings? No, that's not for me."

She expected a lecture about the value of family, but instead, her mother changed the subject entirely. "So tell me about John. Are you still seeing him?"

"No, Mom," Corinne said. "We broke up months ago."

Her mother looked stricken. "Really? You didn't tell me."

"It wasn't relevant."

"To what?"

"To anything."

Her mother looked out over the water, as if sifting this new information.

"Don't look so distraught, Mom. I do go out with a couple of other guys."

"Really?" she asked hopefully. "Tell me about them."

Corinne really didn't want to. Neither of them

was important enough to warrant getting her mother's hopes up, but she'd made the mistake of bringing it up, and she couldn't get out of it now.

"Well, one happens to be a coach at the local high school. He's a nice guy. I'm not that into football."

"What's his name?"

"Simon," she said. "Most everybody calls him Si." She couldn't believe she had mentioned him. They had only been out twice, and he wasn't really her type.

"Si, huh? Interesting name. What about the other one?"

"Well, the other one is an airline pilot who's gone a lot, and I walk his dog. He's pretty cool." She paused and mentally kicked herself. He was even less significant than Simon. "I'm not exactly head over heels for either of them." She slipped off her shoes and socks, then stepped into the water and let it rush around her feet. "I know what you're thinking. You're thinking I'm wasting my time, if I'm not serious about either of them. I enjoy their company when they're with me, and that's enough."

"You don't *want* a relationship?"

Her mother's crestfallen look was almost amusing. "Not really," she said. She crossed her arms, then realized it looked a little self-conscious.

Her mother was gazing pensively at her.

"You don't believe me, do you?" Corinne asked.

"I know you, Corinne. I know when you were a little girl you used to walk around with a doily on your head playing bride. If I've heard it once, I've heard it a million times: 'When I get married . . . when I have children . . .' It's just the last few years that you quit saying it."

"Well, maybe in the last few years I've realized that that's not the be-all and end-all. Maybe I have other goals now. You're the one who taught me to set goals, Mom. And I'm trying not to presume on God. You taught me that, too. If God wants me married, he'll send the husband." She had told herself that so many times that she should have believed it.

"But not all of our goals should be business-oriented," her mother said. "They can't all be about accomplishing things. Sometimes they have to be about relationships, about important bonds. We have to purposely decide to build those, you know. Just like building your businesses."

A big wave washed around her ankles, almost knocking her off her feet. "And how would I go about that, Mom? Do I decide that within two years I'm going to be married? So what do I do then? Go out to bars and start dating everybody who buys me a drink? Or get into singles groups at churches for the sole purpose of meeting a man?"

"A singles group would be nice for you, Corinne. You'd make friends. You'd build relationships."

45

"I'd meet men," she said, "and I have a real big philosophical problem with going to church to meet men."

"But think about it. What kind of a man do you want to meet and marry? The kind you meet in passing, that might be Christian and might not? Or do you want to meet guys who go to church?"

Corinne bent over and scooped a handful of wet sand, then let it fall through her fingers. "I'd like to someday have a Christian husband, if I'm going to have a husband at all," she said. "But I still think it's wrong to go to church looking for one."

She kicked at the water, making a splash. Her mother stood just out of the water's reach. "I just don't want you to be alone. I don't want you to have Christmases like I had this last year." Her voice broke off, and she stepped back to avoid a wave.

Again, Corinne felt the sting of failure. "Mom, I'm so sorry I didn't come home for Christmas. I just had so much going on, and I couldn't see how I could work the time out. I figured Sarah and her brood would be with you. If I'd realized they weren't . . ."

"I understand that," Maggie cut in. "Really, I do. But I'm telling you, I don't want you to have Christmases alone. I don't want you to have to wonder what you're going to eat for Thanksgiving. For one, you and Sarah aren't that close. What are you going to do when I'm gone? It's not like you're going to fly across the country to her house on holidays."

"Not that she'd want me there, anyway," Corinne said.

"I just want you to have people in your life who love you," Maggie said. "I want to know that you have a place of your own. It's very important to me."

"And what if I'm not called to have a family, Mom? What if God has singleness in mind for me? Are you going to be disappointed all your life? Are you going to feel that somehow you've failed with me?"

"Of course not. If I knew that you were getting everything out of life that God has planned for you, then I would be thrilled."

Corinne pulled the hair back from her face and turned into the wind. "But you're not convinced of that."

"Let's just say that I don't see a lot of peace and joy on your face. I see a lot of pride. But you're like a balloon that's just bouncing around in the wind. You need an anchor."

"I *have* an anchor," she said. "I'm a Christian, Mom. I know whom I belong to."

Her mother smiled. "That gives me peace, Corinne. But I'd like to see you anchored to a family, too. I don't want you envying your sister for the rest of your life."

Her mother might as well have thrown ice in her face. "I'm not jealous of her, Mom, if that's what you think." She looked down, trying to seem unaffected, and picked up a seashell. She washed it off in the water and rolled it around in her hand. "You know, not everybody can have the perfect life, like Sarah has. Some of us have to live in the real world." She picked up another seashell, and another. Her mother kept watching her, as if analyzing the pathos behind her words. "Let me off the hook, won't you, Mom? I really don't want to feel bad about myself tonight."

"I make you feel bad about yourself?" she asked.

"Yes," Corinne said, "when you start talking families and husbands and all the things that I don't have." She swallowed. "Makes me feel like a failure."

"How can you possibly think of it as failure?"

"Because *you* do," Corinne said. She picked up another seashell and rinsed the handful off in the water. "I bet I could make some great earrings with these and add them to my collection. I could probably sell them for fifteen or twenty dollars a pop. Maybe tomorrow I'll go to the craft store and see if I can get supplies."

"Beauty into bucks," her mom said softly.

"What?" Corinne asked.

She seemed to shake herself out of her thoughts. "Nothing. You were a good student, Corinne. Too good."

Corinne wasn't sure she understood her mother's sudden melancholy. "Mom, if you're worried that I'm going to spend all my time making jewelry while I'm here, I won't, okay? I promise to give you my undivided attention. You won't have to be disappointed in me."

Not waiting for her mother's response, or pausing to read her expression, Corinne turned away to find more shells.

chapter nine

It had been a bad night for Maggie. She'd had
trouble falling asleep, then had dozed too lightly
to rest. Regrets and recriminations had tugged at
her heart all night, and now, as the morning sun
rose behind the cabin called Seaside, she wondered if it was possible to undo the damage she'd
done to her daughters.

She thought of Corinne's words on the beach
last night. Where had Corinne ever gotten the
idea that she'd disappointed her mother? As
quickly as the question came, she knew the
answer: she'd given Corinne that evidence over
and over in her life. Accomplishments had not
been met with joy and peace and congratulation.
Instead, they'd been met with a question. *What
are you going to do now?* She regretted that. She'd
stolen something important from their childhood, and now their adult lives were bearing wit-
ness to that.

She stepped out onto the deck and sat down
with her coffee. It was nippy out, and a brisk
wind blew up from the water. As she sat there
sipping her coffee, she felt God's presence, as if
he sat next to her like a husband, holding her
hand and easing her pain. He had sent this

March wind, she thought with a smile, and he had ordered every wave that would slap against the shore today. All those sea gulls swooping down over the water and catching their morning meal were cared for and provided for by God.

He would provide for her, as well.

The glass door behind her slid open, and Sarah and Corinne stood in their robes looking out at her, side by side. It reminded her of their childhood Christmas mornings, when the first one up would wake the other, and they'd come find her, their gowns dragging the floor and their bare feet peeking out.

"Something smells good in here, Mom," Corinne said. "What is it?"

"Look in the oven," Maggie said. "It's a breakfast casserole. Why don't you bring it out, and we can share breakfast?"

She loved seeing her girls this early in the morning, before their hair had been sprayed down and their makeup applied. It reminded her of their former innocence — before life had shaped them into adults. Back when their faces were clean and shiny and open, unpretentious.

They brought plates, forks, the casserole, and the pot of coffee and sat down around the table.

"Isn't it nice out?" Maggie asked them.

"It is," Corinne said, her hair wisping into her face. "I don't think I've ever been to Florida when it wasn't sweltering."

"Did you both sleep well?" Maggie asked.

"Well enough," Sarah said, and Maggie recognized the evasion.

"As well as ever," Corinne admitted.

Sarah sipped her coffee. "So, what are we going to do today, Mom?"

A cool wind ruffled Maggie's hair. "Oh, there are so many things I want to do," she said. "I'd like to rent a boat, go out on the ocean, maybe do some fishing. I haven't done that since I was a little girl. There are fishing poles in the storage room. We could pack a picnic and go out to Fork Island and sunbathe."

The girls exchanged a dull stare. "Mom, isn't it a little dangerous for three women to take a boat out when none of us really knows anything about boating?"

"Okay, then," she said, "we can rent a boat and hire someone to sail it for us. That'll be even better."

"Right, Mom," Corinne said.

"Now what's wrong with that?" Maggie asked.

"Nothing," Corinne said. "It just seems like a lot of trouble to put someone to."

"Trouble? Why is it trouble?"

"Well, why would some stranger give us several hours of his day?"

"For money," she said. "I wouldn't have asked him to do it for free."

Sarah rubbed her arms and lifted her shoulders against the wind. "Well, I can't go anywhere until I take care of this printing problem I've got."

"And I have to work on V-Tech's Web site this

morning, Mom," Corinne added. "If I don't, I'm sunk. I depend on the income from it."

Maggie set down her cup. "Well, do you think I can at least have an hour or so of your time after breakfast? I mean, since you did come here to let me take pictures of you?"

"Of course," Corinne said.

"Mom, we can do whatever you want," Sarah said. "There are just a few things we have to take care of first."

Corinne searched Maggie's face, as if gauging her disappointment. "But we can't get them on the phone until eight, anyway, so we might as well go ahead and take pictures," she said. "But Mom, as soon as I get this problem taken care of, I promise I'm yours for the rest of the day."

"And what if you *don't* get it taken care of, Corinne? And you, Sarah? What if you *can't* resolve this in one phone call?"

Sarah sat back hard in her chair. "Well, then, I'll make two phone calls."

Frustrated, Maggie turned to Corinne. "If you can't fix the Web site, are we just going to call this week a wash?"

"Of course not, Mom," Corinne said. "I wouldn't do that. But I told you I was busy when you asked me to come. I told you I had all this work to do and that there were problems."

It was true. They had both warned her. She looked back over the water again and hoped the wind would dry the mist in her eyes before it was obvious to her daughters. "I just had this vision,

I guess, of us running along the beach, kicking at the waves, basking in the sun. I thought we'd laugh and walk and fish . . . then laugh some more. I didn't picture you girls with laptops, or with telephones stuck to your ears."

"I promise, Mom," Corinne said, "it's not going to be like that, okay?"

Maggie knew she was about to cry, so she quickly got up and began to clear the cups. "It's okay," she said. "I understand."

She hated the martyrdom in her voice. The last thing she wanted was to manipulate them. She started into the house, aware of the silence behind her as her daughters stayed at the table.

She went into the kitchen and set the cups into the sink. She stood over it, staring down at them, as if they were somehow to blame.

She had a choice in how she would respond to her daughters' lack of enthusiasm. She could allow it to ruin the week, foil all her plans, and turn the few good moments into guilt moments. Or she could resolve to take what they freely chose to give. Yes. She wanted the gift, not the guilt.

Sarah and Corinne came in after a moment to get dressed. Peeking into their rooms, Maggie could see that, since they knew she was going to be photographing them, they were each taking great pains with their makeup. None of that natural stuff for them. They would each use every resource the cosmetic companies had to offer.

When they were ready, they all went out on the

sand and walked to the water's edge. Maggie backed away from them and they moved together, smiling into the camera. Halfheartedly, she snapped the picture. "I don't want you to pose," she said, lifting her voice over the sound of the surf. "I want to get some spontaneous shots. Splash around in the water or something."

Sarah shot her a look that questioned her sanity. "Mom, I'm not wearing a bathing suit, and if I were, I sure wouldn't let you take a picture of me in it."

"And I'd turn a few cartwheels," Corinne said, "but it's been about ten years since I was a cheerleader."

"So you don't have to act like little kids," her mother said. "I just want you to stop looking at the camera. Stop trying to look beautiful. Just let me do the work."

Chagrined and impatient, they walked along the shore, Sarah pointing out unusual shells, Corinne picking them up. Maggie took a dozen pictures and reloaded, but knew that she still didn't have anything she could use. Their faces were distracted, weary, overdressed. Still — that *was* their natural look. It was who they were, whether she liked it or not.

They turned around and walked back toward the cabin. As they neared it, she could see the glances they stole toward Seaside, as if the solutions to a million problems waited just inside that glass door. Finally, when she ran out of film the second time, she gave them what they wanted. "Go on in, girls. Take care of your business."

Sarah hesitated. "Are you sure, Mom?"

"Of course. Just don't fight over the phone line."

The girls started up to the house, but Maggie hung back.

"Where will you be?" Corinne asked.

"A friend of mine who helped me find this cabin has a photo studio not far from here. He told me I could use his darkroom if I wanted. I think I'll go over there and see what I've got."

"Good idea," Sarah said, relief dripping from her tone. "You can see the fruit of your labor today."

"Instant gratification," Corinne said. "What a concept."

"I doubt that," Maggie said. "I'm not sure I got what I was looking for. But the week is young. There's still time."

She prayed the hope in her words would seep into her heart. She needed to believe it.

chapter ten

Maggie had no trouble finding the studio where Milton was taking pictures of a family with nine-month-old triplets. He looked frazzled and worn, as if he needed a break. She waved to get his attention, and his old face lit up. He stepped over the cords and gave his assistant a few instructions, then came out into the hall and gave Maggie a hug.

"Good to see you, Mags," he said, kissing her cheek. "So how's it going over at Seaside?"

"Oh, as well as I should have expected," she said. "But I took a couple of rolls this morning and I thought I'd see how they came out, if you can spare the darkroom."

"It's all yours," he said, and led her up the hall. He opened the door, let her in, and stood leaning against the casing. "Think you got what you were hoping for?"

She tried to smile. "Let's just say we're having a little trouble getting started."

"Well, I'll be praying for you," he said.

"Thanks, Milton."

"And take as long as you need in here," he said. "I won't be coming anywhere near this place for the next few days. I'm booked solid with sittings. Someday I'll have the nerve to retire."

"You're a lifesaver," she said. "I really appreciate it."

He closed her in and she turned on the red light that enabled her to see what she was doing.

A little while later, she stood over the developing trays as the faces began to emerge on her prints. She stared down at them, like a new mother straining for the first glimpse of her child's face.

As each one of the prints came into focus, she realized that her expectations had been on target. She had wanted to see joy in her girls' faces, peace and love and abundance of life. But what she saw, instead, was more honest than that. It was who they really were. She saw anxiety and lines of weariness, distraction, and discontent.

She hung the pictures on the line above her and walked from one end of the room to the other, examining the shots one by one. She had taught them everything she'd known. But she hadn't *known* the right things.

She closed her eyes and prayed for those faces that meant more to her than life itself — although she doubted that they knew that.

Her heart ached for prints of bright eyes and soaring spirits. "Lord," she whispered, "don't let them miss the abundance, the joy, the peace. If you could just give me a few little miracles."

As she drove back to the cabin, she reminded herself that miracles were right up God's alley. Maybe he would help her with this, after all.

chapter eleven

While her mother was gone, Sarah spent thirty minutes on the telephone with the printer, trying to convince him that the church shouldn't have to pay to have the printing done again. By the time she got off, she'd gotten him to cut the price of the second printing in half. It was better than nothing, even if she had to eat the cost herself.

She hung up and called Jim at work to ask him to go by and proofread the new copy. But he was still angry at her.

"Come on, Jim," she said, "don't do this to me when I'm away from home and I can't do anything about it."

"I'm not doing anything to you, Sarah. You're doing it to me. You're the one who lambasted me for what I fed the kids for supper last night. And, by the way, they were still alive when I woke them up this morning. The pie didn't kill them."

She had lain awake all night, running their conversation back through her mind, and in the end had had to admit to herself that her tone with him had been controlling and condescending. She didn't blame him for being angry.

"I'm sorry about last night, Jim. I went overboard. I was tense."

If he accepted her apology, he didn't say so.

"If you want me to get someone else to go by the printer's," she said, "I will. I can call Dana or Mary. I just trust you to catch any mistakes."

"I'll go by there," he said, "but I'm not fighting your battles for you. I have enough of my own to fight."

"There's no battle to fight," she said. "I've already worked it all out with him. Just proofread it and make sure everything is spelled right."

"Tell you what. Why don't I just fax you a copy so you can do it? I don't want to be responsible for this if I overlook something."

"Okay, fine," she said. "Hold on a minute." She left the bedroom and went into the living room where Corinne was pounding furiously on her laptop keys. "Corinne, do you have a fax on that computer?"

"Yes," her sister clipped, "except that I can't use it because you're tying up the phone line."

Sarah set her hands on her hips. "I have to take care of something!"

"Well, so do I," Corinne said, "only I can't get online until you get off the phone."

Sarah just stared down at her. "Why are you so hostile?"

"I'm not hostile! I just need a stinking phone line!"

"Okay, I'm getting off! Is there any possibility that I can get Jim to fax me something through your computer?"

"He can try — on the off chance that the phone isn't busy."

Huffing at her sister's tone, Sarah talked to Jim briefly and hung up. "He's going to fax it to me in an hour," she told Corinne stiffly. "Phone's all yours for now. Knock yourself out." Sarah looked in the refrigerator, but found nothing that interested her. When she turned back to Corinne, her sister was sifting through her briefcase. "Well, are you going to use it or not? Because I have some other calls to make —"

"I'm looking for my modem cord," Corinne snapped. "I have to plug my computer in." She jerked the cord out of her briefcase and pulled the phone off the wall. Jabbing her modem cord into the jack, she muttered, "It's hard enough to do this when I can't talk to them on the phone and get online at the same time. Probably doesn't matter, anyway. They've probably already fired me because I couldn't get a stupid phone line."

"You could have asked," Sarah said.

"No, I couldn't," she told her. "You were too busy yelling at that printer guy. You couldn't *hear* me."

"Well, you're wasting time now. Go ahead and do it, for heaven's sake." Sarah watched as Corinne punched the keys, her mouth tight. Corinne had dark circles under her eyes. Sarah wondered if she had slept last night. Sarah had awakened several times during the night and heard movement in the living room. Had

Corinne been up all night working?

She felt guilty for being so hard on her sister. "Want a cup of coffee?"

Corinne looked up, surprised. "Yeah, I could use one."

"Why didn't you sleep last night?"

Corinne kept typing and shook her head. "I was too worried about this Web site. I can't figure out what's going wrong. Customers can shop, but they can't check out. And when I was trying to fix it, I accidentally dumped some critical stuff. If they were mad before, they're going to be livid now."

"But you have two other businesses, right?"

"Those two other businesses bring in peanuts compared to this. And I think I've got it worked out if I can just upload it and see if it works."

Sarah got Corinne her coffee, then left her alone to work. She got her legal pad on which she loved to make lists, and took it out on the deck so she wouldn't distract her sister. She started making notes about all the things she needed to do as soon as she could get the phone line back. Maybe she should go to a pay phone, make a few phone calls, take care of some things without butting heads with her sister. But soon her mother would be back, and she didn't want to be gone when she arrived. Her mother had been melancholy enough when she'd left this morning.

After a while, she went back in and heard Corinne on the telephone talking to the client she was so worried about. Corinne sounded as if she had corrected the problem. Sarah hoped it would improve her mood.

As soon as Corinne was off the phone, Sarah reached for it. "You're not about to use that, are you?" Corinne snapped.

Sarah froze. "I thought I would. Why?"

"Because I'm waiting for them to call me back if they need to. This is real business, Sarah."

Sarah crossed her arms and gave her sister a sullen look. "And what exactly constitutes 'real business?' Is it that you get paid for doing it?"

"Well, yeah, that's a biggie," Corinne said. "Bills to pay and all that."

Sarah looked at the ceiling, as if it was all clearly laid out there. "So the work I do, including taking care of my home, my family, the literacy program, the church work, the PTA, all of those things are not 'real' business because I don't net a paycheck, is that it?"

"If your things don't get done, you have a backup. You have a husband that can go and do them behind you. I don't have anybody like that. I have clients that count on me to do the work, and if I don't do it, then they'll find other people who can."

Sarah groaned and started for the door.

"Where are you going?"

"I'm going to find a pay phone," Sarah said. "I have business to take care of whether I'm being paid for it or not — whether *anybody* on the face of this earth *appreciates* it or not. I made a commitment to do it and I'm going to. So when

Mom gets back, tell her I'll be back as soon as I can get these phone calls made."

Corinne threw up her hands. "She'll ask why you didn't just make them from here!"

"Well, why don't *you* just explain it to her?" Sarah bellowed back, and slammed the door behind her.

Sarah started across the sand, looking for a pay phone somewhere on the beach. If she walked far enough back toward town, maybe her cell phone would pick up a signal. Leave it to her mother to find a place so private and remote that it didn't have commercial businesses or even other cabins close by. Sarah feared that she'd have a long walk before she had any luck. But she had taken only a few steps when she saw her mother's rental car pulling back into the driveway. Sarah waited as her mother got out of the car and came around the house.

"Sarah, where are you going?"

"I was looking for a phone," she said. "Or trying to get a cell signal."

"What's wrong with the phone in the house?"

"Corinne doesn't want me using it," she said. "She considers her business to be more important than mine, you know? Paycheck and all? So I thought I would walk down the beach and find a pay phone."

"Oh, Sarah, come in the house."

"Mom, I really need to take care of these things."

"Well, then take the car in a little while and

find a pay phone, but don't take off walking aimlessly like some little kid running away from home."

Feeling like a reprimanded child, Sarah charged up the steps of the deck and headed in through the back door, her mother trailing behind her. Corinne looked up at them from her computer, with that look on her face she used to get when she'd been caught harassing her sister. "Hi, Mom."

"Corinne, what is this about you not letting your sister use the phone?"

"*Letting* her use the phone?" Corinne shot back. "She's been on it since you left. I've just been sitting here pounding on these keys and biting my tongue."

"You're grown women," Maggie said. "I refuse to referee like I did when you were kids." She slapped an envelope down on the table. The pictures spilled out. "So you two just fight it out and make your phone calls and do your business, and I'll find something to occupy myself." With that, she headed to the back bedroom and closed the door.

Because no one seemed to be in the mood to go out to eat, Sarah found some cans of tuna and made sandwiches for all of them. They avoided each other for the rest of the day, Maggie watching old movies in her bedroom, Corinne glued to her laptop, and Sarah making an occasional phone call back home to make sure that her volunteers were doing everything necessary before the prayer conference.

Midafternoon, Corinne took a break and drifted over to the snapshots her mother had taken that morning. "These are awful," she said, sorting through them. "No wonder Mom's so upset."

Sarah came to the table and gave them a cursory glance. "I look like death warmed over. What did she expect at seven in the morning?"

"It's not the time of day," Corinne said. "Neither one of us had our heart in it."

"Well, my heart's *never* into getting my picture taken. It's not my favorite thing to do."

"But that's why Mom brought us here," Corinne said. "We should have tried a little harder."

"We can try harder tomorrow," she said. "I think today's a washout."

Corinne went to the window and let her gaze drift out to the shore. Clouds hung low in the sky, and a strong wind stirred up the sea. Angry, foaming waves slammed against the sand. She knew that her mother was just as angry on the other side of that bedroom door. She hated herself for contributing to that, but she didn't know how to fix it. Besides, her mother always got over it. Tomorrow they could do things right. As Sarah had said, tomorrow they could make a fresh start.

A storm moved in that afternoon, and it rained

for hours. Corinne used the time to sleep, since she hadn't rested well the night before. Sarah solved a few crises over the phone, then went into her mother's room to watch a movie with her.

The phone rang several times during the evening, and was always for either Corinne or Sarah. With each telephone ring, Maggie seemed to get more and more distant. Finally, she claimed to be tired and went to bed early. One by one, they each turned in, deciding that this day wasn't worth salvaging, that maybe by tomorrow the rain would have stopped, the clouds would have passed on, and things would look a little better.

chapter twelve

The storm raged on through the night, and Maggie had trouble sleeping again. Thunder cracked outside her window, and the waves pounded the shore. Maybe it was a sign, she thought. She had felt such peace at home before she came here. She had fooled herself into thinking that the peace would just drip off her onto her children, that they would sense that things were different. But the girls were too caught up in their own problems. She couldn't stand another few days of keeping them imprisoned here when it was the last place they wanted to be.

Maybe it had all been a mistake.

She waited until dawn yellowed the dark of the sky, and then she made a decision. She would release them from the vacation, and if they wanted to go home, they could. In fact, she would even help them.

She went into Sarah's bedroom. Her daughter was still sleeping soundly. Maggie moved quietly, careful not to wake her. She pulled out the drawers and began to drop Sarah's clothes into her suitcase. As she gathered up shoes and underwear and toiletries, she began to cry. Sarah hadn't brought much, because Maggie had taught her to pack light. But if it was already packed, then Sarah wouldn't have to wait another moment to head back home.

When she'd finished with Sarah, she went into Corinne's room and packed up her things. Then she went back into the kitchen and sat down with her coffee, staring out the glass to the ocean beyond. So much majesty out there, she thought, as the sun came up and painted the sky gold. So much power in those angry waves — yet Maggie herself felt so small and had so little. What would she do later this morning, when both of her daughters were gone? Should she pack and leave, or stay and try to enjoy the quiet?

She didn't think she had the heart to do that alone.

She rose and stepped closer to the window. There was a lone sailboat near the horizon, moving slowly across the water, as if it was in no hurry. She wondered if it had come through the storm, or if it had waited for it to end, then launched out in its aftermath.

She longed to show her daughters that kind of unhurried pace.

It wasn't long before she heard Sarah moving around in the bedroom, no doubt looking for her things. After a moment, she came to the bedroom door and looked out.

"Mom?"

Maggie turned from the window. "Good morning."

"Morning," Sarah said. "I was looking for my things. Did you pack them?"

"Yes, I did." Maggie turned back to the sail-boat, still rocking on the waves.

"But, Mom!"

She heard Corinne opening her door and stepping out into the family room. "She packed mine, too," she told Sarah. "Mom, what's going on?"

Maggie turned to her rumpled, groggy daughters and tried to hold back her tears. She could do this. She could go back to her stoic facade, the one she'd worn so often when they were growing up, the one that had contributed to who they were today. "I decided to let you both go," she said. "There's no point in keeping you trapped here. Your plane tickets can be changed, and if there's any problem, I'll pay the difference."

"Go back home?" Sarah asked. "Why? We've only been here two days."

"Well, you don't need five more like these two," Maggie said. "Let's face it. It was a failed experiment."

Corinne leaned against the wall, looking sleepy and bewildered. "Experiment? Mom, it was a vacation."

"No, it wasn't," Maggie said. "It was never a vacation. You don't have time for a vacation." She hated herself when she couldn't control the emotion taking over her face or keep her voice level. "There's cereal to eat and milk. But you

71

don't have to wait around. I can get you back to the airport as soon as you want. I even called for the flight times. They're over there on the table."

Neither of her daughters made a move to look at the flight schedule. Maggie searched the horizon again and found that sailboat. She wondered about the person sailing out there. Did he have children who understood about floating idly with no place to go? Had he taught them that peace, or had he learned it too late?

"Mom, we don't have to go home," Sarah said.

"No," Corinne agreed. "We want to stay. We want to spend time with you."

Maggie started to laugh. Turning back to her daughters, she said, "Give me a break."

Sarah shot Corinne a condemning look. Corinne returned it.

Sarah started to cry. "Mom, I'm so sorry I messed up the week," she said. "I just had so much on my mind. It was a really bad time for me."

Maggie pulled out a chair and sat down at the table. The box she had brought of old pictures, the ones she had hoped they would put into photo albums, was right in the middle of the table. She wiped her face and pulled the box closer, dumping the pictures out. She shifted through until she found one taken when the girls were three and eight. They'd been so sweet, so innocent. There had actually been peace and joy on their faces then.

"When did it change?" she asked out loud.

"When did what change?" Sarah asked.

"Everything," she said. "Look at these pictures. Look at your faces." She reached for the pictures she had taken yesterday and compared. "What happened?"

Sarah pulled out a chair and lowered herself into it. "We became adults, Mom. We have responsibilities. Back then we didn't have to make any decisions. We didn't have to be useful."

"That's it," Maggie said. "Useful. That's what I taught you, isn't it? I taught you how to overachieve and how to get things done. I taught you how to accomplish things. But I didn't teach either one of you how to be happy."

Corinne met Sarah's eyes, and slowly she lowered herself into the chair next to her mother. "Mom, I'm happy," she said, though her tone belied it. "Sarah is, too, aren't you, Sarah?"

"I am, Mom."

"See, that's the thing," Maggie said, reaching out to take both of their hands. "I think you both *think* you're happy. You really do. You just don't know any better. But the way you snipe at each other, the worry on both of your faces, the anxiety, the inability to rest." She looked from one of her girls to the other. "You know, I sometimes think that if it weren't for me, you two would never see each other again. You'd go the rest of your lives without ever getting in touch with each other."

"Of course that's not true," Sarah said.

"What if I wasn't here anymore?" Maggie asked Corinne. "Would you go visit Sarah? Would you get to know her kids? Or would you just withdraw completely and try to get along without any hint of your past, of our little family?"

"I'd go to Sarah's, if she invited me," Corinne said weakly, but Maggie knew she didn't mean it.

"Of course, I'd invite you," Sarah said. "Why wouldn't I invite you? You're my sister."

Maggie shook her head. "No, I think the family would be torn apart. There wouldn't be much left. Not of this family right here, the one that we represented. There's too much anger, too much resentment."

She regarded her younger daughter. That vulnerable expression made her look years younger than she was. "I don't know why you've been so mad at Sarah all these years, Corinne. And, Sarah, I don't know why you're always so aggravated with Corinne. Maybe it's just a response. I don't know what it is. But I don't really have the energy to work it all out. I want you both to go home today. I want you to take your suitcases and get in that rental car and head back to the airport."

Corinne started to cry then, and she rested her forehead on her fist. "I'm not going, Mom."

Maggie patted her shoulder. "Yes, you are. And it's okay, Corinne. It's my idea."

"But I'm not going," Corinne said again. "I'm

staying. I said I would, and I will. And in this family we always keep our promises, don't we?"

"That's another thing I taught you."

Sarah's frustration shone in her eyes. "That's a good thing, Mom."

"Yeah, it's a good thing," she said, "but I only said it so many times to punctuate your father's inability to keep *his* promises. It was just one way of getting a little dig at him. So now we all keep our promises, if it kills us. We fulfill our obligations, even when they don't make sense. And as we do, we focus on the obligations themselves, not any joy they bring us or anyone else. Because none of them really bring any joy." She squeezed their hands and looked back out the glass doors. The boat was still there, swaying on the rhythm of the waves. "I want to be like that," she whispered. "Out there with no place to go. No hurry. No telephones. No schedule. But that's not what brings you girls happiness. And I don't want this week to be another joyless obligation."

Sarah looked through her tears at the boat she hadn't noticed before. "I'm not going, either," Sarah said. Her eyes locked with Corinne's as if making a pact.

Corinne's voice wobbled as words choked out. "Mom, I hope you can forgive me for the way I've acted. And Sarah, I know it seems that I don't think much of you, but that's not true. I think a lot of you. I always have. You were the pretty one, the smart one. I had to come up in your shadow. All the teachers knew who you were. You have a great husband, a beautiful home. You had the first children. You have such a full life. It's so different from mine. And I admit . . . I'm a little jealous."

Sarah looked stunned, and Corinne met her mother's eyes. "Mom's known it for a long time now. She's brought it up, and I've denied it. But the truth is I am really, really jealous of you, Sarah. I want what you have, and it doesn't seem to be happening for me."

"What *I* have?" Sarah asked. "Corinne, you've got to be kidding. Look at you. You weigh the same thing you weighed when you graduated from high school. You're still so young and pretty. Life hasn't left marks on you like it has on me. I have a body that clearly shows that I've had two children, and I can't lose weight to save my life."

"You don't *need* to lose weight," Maggie said.

"Well, I don't weigh what I weighed in high school," Sarah told her. "And I wish I did. I look at Corinne and I see how free she is and how she doesn't have all the things tugging on her that I have." She held out her hand to stop Corinne's protest. "And I don't mean that to diminish your businesses, Corinne. I envy you for being able to follow all of your dreams and to carry them out. I've never *ever* heard you say you wanted to do something that you didn't wind up doing."

"Oh, please," Corinne said. "You make me sound like a super businesswoman."

Sarah shook her head. "No, *you* make you

sound like that. I'm just agreeing."

"Well, it's all a lie," Corinne spouted. "I'm not any super businesswoman. The truth is, I can hardly pay my bills. Some months I have to put my rent payment on a credit card. I work so hard because I don't have a choice. Yeah, there's some satisfaction in making things succeed, but the truth is, I have to eat, and that's why I've been scared to death of losing this account. My whole business might go under if I lose it. And I'm stressed out and exhausted all the time. I *always* have insomnia. I'm on this endless cycle of working on the Internet, walking dogs, doing jewelry parties. And you wonder why I don't have any relationships. Well, how could I? *When* could I? And who in his right mind would want to spend time with a woman with debts up to her ears, who can never make ends meet and can't clear her schedule long enough to eat a decent meal?"

Maggie sat back hard in her chair. "Well, at least now we're getting somewhere," she said. "Corinne, do you know I felt like you're feeling most of my life? We can't all have lives like Sarah."

Sarah slapped her hands on the table. "Stop it! Lives like Sarah? If you only knew." She got to her feet and walked around the table, her arms crossed. She went to the sliding glass doors and stared out with dull eyes. "The truth is, one of the reasons I've been making so many phone calls home is that Jim is hardly speaking to me, and I've been trying to smooth things over."

"Not speaking to you?" Maggie asked. "Well, what's the matter?"

"I'm not even sure. I'm too controlling, and I complain all the time. He's fed up, I guess. My marriage is on the rocks. My kids hate me because I don't feed them pie for supper and throw a party every night. And this prayer conference and the literacy program are things that validate me. They're things I can do and do well, and get a few pats on the back for, because I don't get that many at home. All I've ever really wanted was approval, from you, Mom, or from Dad, wherever he was. But the truth is that the harder I work, the less appreciated I feel. And if I mess up just once, if I drop the ball, everybody in my life will just . . ." Her voice trailed off.

"Just what?" Maggie prompted.

"Just vanish," she choked. "They'll just get up and leave."

"Sarah!" Corinne said. "Your children aren't going to leave you."

"Neither is Jim," Maggie threw in.

"I don't know," she said, turning back to the glass. "You didn't hear him on the phone the other night when he was feeding them dessert for dinner and they were thrilled and laughing and celebrating. 'Ding, dong, the witch is dead.' "

"Oh, it wasn't like that, honey," Maggie said. "They're just having fun being with their dad."

"Being with their dad without me," she said. "So where does that leave me? When I get home, what do I do? Do I shirk all my responsibilities as their mother and start indulging them just so they'll think I'm a fun mom?" She turned back to Corinne. "It's not like you think it is. My life is not perfect. It's far from perfect. In fact, if I manage to smooth things over with Jim and get a smile back on his face when he looks at me, it'll be a real miracle, because I don't remember the last time that happened. I haven't seen that smile in a very long time."

She stood there as tears started to stream down her face, and Maggie and Corinne both sat there staring up at her. As if it occurred to them at the same time, they both got up and put their arms around her in the first real family hug they'd had in years. They clung to each other, sister to sister, mother to daughter, weeping their hearts out for all the ugly things they had brought here with them.

"I don't want to go home, Mom," Sarah said. "I want to experience whatever it is you wanted me to experience here."

"Me, too," Corinne said. "We want to stay, Mom."

Their tears were like healing balm to Maggie. "Okay," she said finally. "If you stay because you want to and not because you have to."

"We are," Sarah said.

"Promise," Corinne agreed.

When they had finished unpacking, it began to rain again. They went out to breakfast, and Maggie insisted that no one count calories, that they eat what they wanted and all they wanted. When they got back, they set about working on the photo albums that she had brought, and started sorting their family pictures into years.

And as they did, the turns in the road became clearer.

chapter thirteen

Maggie watched Corinne staring down at the snapshot in her hand: her mother and father when they were no more than eighteen or nineteen. In the photo, Maggie had on a short wedding veil and a white suit and carried a bouquet of flowers. Corinne's father, standing next to Maggie, looked debonair and proud in his tux. Maggie shook her head. Knowing what she knew of the rest of their lives, it was hard for her to believe they had ever been in love.

"What you got?" Sarah asked. "Oh, look, Mom, your wedding. I didn't know you still had pictures of Dad. I thought you'd cut his head out of all of them."

Maggie smirked. "I kept some, hidden away."

"Why?" Corinne's question was sincere and serious. "You hated him so."

"I didn't hate him," Maggie said. When she saw their disbelieving looks, she knew there was no point in denying the truth. "Well, okay, I did. But I don't anymore."

"It's easy to quit hating people after they're dead," Sarah pointed out.

"Yeah, it's easy to forgive when they aren't around to test you," Maggie said. "But believe it or not, one of my biggest regrets in life is that I allowed myself to hate him, and I made sure you both knew it." Maggie studied Corinne's soft look as she gazed at her father's image. "Maybe I should have talked him up like some kind of absent hero. Maybe I should have allowed you girls your fantasies about him pining away for his little princesses."

"Mom, we would have realized the truth, eventually," Sarah whispered. "When he only called us on our birthdays and Christmas. When he talked about his stepchildren like they were his flesh and blood, instead of us. When he had no desire to see us, or know anything at all about us."

"And you had been so hurt," Corinne said. "You did the best you could, Mom. You had reason to be bitter."

"Maybe," Maggie said. "But the bitterness hurt me, not him. If I'd forgiven him, I could have moved on. And your lives might have been different. When your dad left me, it motivated me to show him, to show everybody, that I could be somebody because I didn't *feel* like anybody. I wanted to show everybody that I was productive and worthwhile."

She sorted through the pictures until she came to the envelope of shots taken two years ago, when she had been in Israel. She flipped through some of the pictures and found the one of her baptism in the Jordan River. She had been in Israel on assignment for a travel magazine, taking pictures of some of the sights with the tour group she'd gone with.

"You know, it wasn't until this trip a couple of years ago that I finally understood what usefulness really is." She got up and moved around the table to bend down between her daughters so they could both study the picture with her. The pastor who had led the tour group had taken her out into the water and baptized her just as Jesus had been.

"When I walked where Jesus walked and saw the things that he saw, I can't tell you the peace that came over me. It was like that dove that flew down on his shoulder when he was baptized and said, 'This is my beloved Son in whom I am well pleased.' I felt like that — like that dove just came down on me and cleansed me of all the past stuff that had gone on in my life, and made me rest, finally, in his peace. All the anger and bitterness vanished."

"That's good, Mama," Corinne whispered. "But you've been a good Christian for as far back as I can remember."

"But something different happened on that trip. I understood. Have you ever come to a rocky place in your life, a place where you don't know if just over the horizon there's a valley or a cliff? If you're going to fall off altogether, or have another mountain to climb?"

Sarah studied her. "Have you been through a rocky place, Mom?"

She met her daughter's eyes, considering

whether now was the time. She didn't feel ready, but Sarah's question couldn't be ignored.

Corinne looked up. Maggie knew that her silence was answering their question. Finally, she pulled the chair around between them. They both turned to face her, waiting. "Today's the day of confessions," she said. "Sarah confessing her marital problems, Corinne confessing that she can't make ends meet. Well, girls, I guess it's time for my confession."

"You're jealous of both of us?" Corinne guessed with a half smile.

Maggie smiled, but her eyes began to glisten. "No, honey, that's not it," she said. "My confession is about why I really brought you here this week."

The girls sat in silent, uneasy anticipation. Maggie knew it was nothing like the silence on the sailboat she'd seen this morning.

"A little over a year ago," she said, "I was diagnosed with ovarian cancer."

They both sat stiffer, and their faces changed. "No way!" Corinne said.

"Mom, you wouldn't keep that from us," Sarah accused.

"Just listen," Maggie said, struggling to keep her voice calm. "At first there were no symptoms. They discovered it in a routine exam. I had surgery and everything was fine."

"Surgery? Mom, you never said —"

"They thought they got it all," Maggie cut in. "But then we discovered that it was in my lymph nodes and in my lung. And there are masses on my kidney — and my pancreas."

Sarah got to her feet, pressing her hand on her forehead. Corinne looked as if she might faint. "Mom, no!" Sarah squeaked out.

Maggie squeezed her hand. "Just listen. Just let me finish."

"Mom, are you going to die?" Corinne blurted.

Maggie couldn't answer that, not yet. "Honey, I went through chemo for over a year. Several different treatments."

"Chemo?" Corinne asked, slowly getting up to join her sister, as if she couldn't hear this alone. "Mom, why wouldn't you tell us? Why wouldn't you let us be there to help you?"

"I had friends helping me," she said, "and I didn't want to worry you. I was sure that the chemo would get rid of the cancer and that I'd be cured. That's why I didn't argue too much about you coming to see me for the last year. My hair had fallen out, and I didn't want you to see me like that. I knew if you found out, you'd worry yourselves sick."

Sarah touched her mother's short-cropped cut. "So that's why your hair is so short?"

Maggie brought her hand up to her hair. "It's just now growing back in."

Sarah's face twisted, and she threw her arms around her. "Oh, Mom!" Corinne put her arms around them both. Maggie felt the emotion coursing through them.

"But the chemo got it all, didn't it?" Corinne choked. "I mean, you don't have to fight this anymore. You're okay, aren't you?"

Maggie wanted nothing more than to tell her that she was right, that it was all over, behind her, that they didn't have to fear it anymore.

But she couldn't.

"No, honey. The chemo didn't work," she said. "And then I went through several other experimental treatments, but the cancer has kept spreading. Things don't look good."

"No!" Corinne backed away. "Mom, you can't just give up. You can't just stop trying!"

"Honey, we've run out of options and it's spreading too fast. I can't hold out false hope. There comes a point when you're just battle-weary. When you've exhausted every possibility, and it's too heavy to hold anymore. That's when you give it over to God. When you start reaching for him, instead of a cure. And you find that he's been there all along, living it with you. It gives you peace. If it's my time, it's my time. God's known it from the very foundation of the world. The only thing I don't have peace about is my relationship with you two, and your relationships with each other. That's why I wanted this week with you. I wanted to set some things right. It was very important for me to do that."

"Mom, you're not dying," Corinne said. "Please tell us you're not dying! There must be something else to try. There must be other doctors."

"We've tried everything, Corinne," she said. "And frankly, I'm tired of fighting. I don't want to be sick anymore. I trust God's sovereignty in this."

"But God gave us drugs!" Sarah cried. "Mom, you need a second opinion. You need a *third* opinion."

"I've had so many doctors poking and prodding me that I'm fed up." She got up and touched Sarah's shoulders. "Honey, it's going to be okay."

"It's not okay!" Sarah said, shaking her off. "It's not okay for my mother to say that she's dying and there's nothing that can be done! I won't believe that. I *will not* believe it!"

"Me, either," Corinne said in a rapid-fire voice. "Mom, we're going to beat this. We're going to figure out something and we're going to beat it. You just need a new doctor. You need somebody more progressive."

"I have very progressive doctors. I've been to the Mayo Clinic and talked to doctors doing trials at several hospitals across the country. They all agree that not much more can be done."

"But they don't just give up!" Corinne cried. "They've got to keep trying, right up until the day . . ."

Her voice trailed off, and Sarah shook her head frantically. *"Oh, no, you are not going to die, Mom! You are not going to die!"*

All at once, Maggie felt as tired as she had after that last chemo treatment. She sat back down and ran her hands over her face. "I don't want to go until I know you've found peace — *not* more stress! Do you understand me? No more stress. I taught you to run the treadmill, and now I want to teach you how to get off. That's what this week is about. Not angsting over my cancer!"

She hated the pain on their faces. She wished she could banish it. "Oh, come here."

They both bent down and clung to her like children being cruelly torn from their parent.

"I don't care what you say," Sarah whispered. "You're not going to die. I won't let you."

It would take some time, but when the moment came to let her go, she hoped they would be ready.

chapter fourteen

The rest of the day was intense and packed with emotion, but neither Corinne nor Sarah tried to take care of business back home. They gave their mother their undivided attention, though they found it hard to fake the joy she had so wanted to find on their faces as she photographed them. Maggie was getting honest emotions, but they weren't the ones she'd hoped for.

When Maggie finally went to bed, Corinne's pain erupted, and she shoved open the glass doors and rushed across the sand to the water. Sarah waited a moment, struggling with her own anguish, then followed. They stood barefoot on the wet sand as the water teased close to them. Side by side, they wept and stared out at the turbulent Gulf.

Sarah set her arm across her sister's shoulder. She couldn't remember the last time she had played the big sister role. For the last several years they had been at such odds with each other that there had been nothing but contempt between them. Too much sibling rivalry, not enough sisterly love. After a moment, Corinne returned the embrace.

Moments ticked by as they stood and cried,

then finally Sarah dropped onto the wet sand, paying no regard to her jeans getting wet or the waves lapping around her feet.

The moonlight was bright on the water, making it twinkle like a million stars. Sarah began to write in the wet sand.

"What are you writing?" Corinne asked.

"I'm making a list," she said. "Things we have to do tomorrow. First, I'll call an oncologist friend back home. He can give me information about this cancer. Maybe he can get the records from Mom's doctor and make sure they're doing the right things. He's up on all the latest treatments. And if there's any place we can take her, any place at all that she can go . . ."

"Right," Corinne cut in, catching her vision. "And I'll get online and find everything I can about this type of cancer and all the treatments available. Information is what we need. Lots of information. Doctors post research results, even if they aren't published in medical journals."

Sarah wrote that on the sand list. "And then we'll go to the bookstore and we'll look for books, and we'll get something on nutrition. I don't think Mom's eating right. I've heard that nutrition plays a big part in fighting cancer."

"That's right," Corinne said. "We can go to the health food store. Get her vitamins. And she needs to see a naturopathic doctor to start her on a regimen."

Sarah jotted health food store and NP doctor on her list.

"Maybe Mom could come home and live with one of us, and we could take care of her. Maybe she needs more surgery. Whatever she needs, we can do it."

But as Sarah started to add that to her list, a large, smashing wave slapped over her, soaking them both. As the water retreated, Sarah looked down at the list. The water had erased it. Tears came to her eyes as the reality of her helplessness washed over her. "Look at me," she said, her words barely audible over the roar of the sea. "I'm making a list in the sand."

Corinne sat staring at the spot where the list had so easily yielded to the tide. The clouds had moved on with today's storm, and a sky full of stars twinkled down over them, their reflection rippling like diamonds.

"We just have to have faith," Sarah whispered.

"Mom has faith, but she's still dying."

"But her faith hasn't failed," Sarah said. "She's still got so much."

"But what in?" Corinne asked her. "It's not in her healing."

"No," Sarah whispered. "She doesn't even seem to be praying for healing."

"Her prayers are for us." Corinne wiped the tears on her face.

Sarah pulled her sister close and held her, and they both wept as the sounds of the ocean muffled their pain, and the waves lapped at the list on the shore.

chapter fifteen

Maggie woke to the sound of voices outside her bedroom window, and she pulled herself out of bed and looked out. Sarah had the phone cord stretched out to the deck, and Maggie wondered if she was having an early argument with Jim. She looked at the clock: seven a.m. She normally woke around five, but unburdening herself to her children had exhausted her, and she had slept more deeply last night than she had in weeks.

She quickly dressed and went into the kitchen. Corinne sat at her computer, banging on the keyboard. Maggie's hopes plummeted. "I thought you weren't going to work today," she said in a dull voice.

Corinne looked up. It was clear from the circles under her eyes that she hadn't slept much. "Morning, Mom." She put her computer down and came to give her a hug. "How are you feeling?"

Maggie waved her away. "I'm fine. Slept like a baby."

"Well, come sit down and I'll get you a cup of coffee."

"I can get myself a cup," Maggie said.

Corinne ignored her and poured a cup, fixed it

the way Maggie liked, then went back to the computer. "I'm not working, by the way. I was doing some research."

"Research? About what?"

"About the kind of cancer you have. I searched the Web and found out that there's some new breakthrough research going on at Duke. You might qualify to be in the study."

Maggie set the coffee mug down hard, sloshing some out. "Corinne, why don't you believe me when I tell you that I've already looked into every possibility? You don't know how long I've been chasing this rabbit."

"It's not a rabbit, Mom. It's your life! New things come up all the time."

"Corinne, I don't have the energy for new things." She sipped her coffee and tried to change the subject. "Now who is your sister talking to?"

Corinne averted her eyes and went back to banging on her computer keyboard. "Nobody. I don't know."

"It's about the cancer, too, isn't it?"

Corinne just looked up at her. Sighing and clutching her coffee cup, Maggie went to the back door and stepped out. Sarah's back was to her, and she apparently didn't hear Maggie approaching. She was speaking with even more passion than she had when she was yelling at the printer about the misspelled word.

"Keith, you must know of something else. Yes, it's in the other organs. Yeah, I can probably do that. She's not being very cooperative, though. Canada? Sure, we could get her there. What kind of alternative treatment?"

Maggie couldn't believe that both daughters were knee-deep in this quagmire that she had resolved to pull herself out of. "Sarah," she said, and Sarah swung around, startled.

"Mom, I didn't know you were awake." She put her hand over the phone. "Did you sleep well?"

"Yes," she said. "Sarah, who are you talking to?"

"Keith Simpson. He's an oncologist friend of mine, Mom. I called him at home."

Maggie considered going back to bed. She sat down on a bench with a thud, suddenly weary. "Let me talk to him."

"But Mom —"

"Let me talk to him," she insisted.

Reluctantly, Sarah gave up the telephone.

Maggie put it to her ear. "Dr. Simpson?"

"Yes," he said.

"Hi, Maggie Downing here. Look, I appreciate your talking to my daughter, especially when she hysterically called you at home this early in the morning. I'm sure she's forgotten that it's six your time."

"That's all right," he said. "I understand her concern."

"Well, the truth is, I have very good doctors. I've been to the Mayo Clinic, I've been to Johns Hopkins, I've been turned down for the trials at

94

Duke and Harvard. I've at least looked into every alternative medical facility I can, and for the last few months I've been on a very strict, healthy diet. I've had surgery, and I've been through over a dozen rounds of very aggressive chemo, and also radiation. The cancer has still spread. It's in more than a few organs, and there's really nothing more they can do. I've accepted that, but obviously my girls need more time."

"Can you blame them?" he asked.

"No, of course I can't blame them. But my point is that I doubt there's anything new that you could offer in the way of hope."

"I'd like to study your case if you wouldn't mind. I could call your doctor and get your records. Sarah and Jim are good friends. I want to help if I can."

Maggie looked at Sarah and knew that she hadn't slept last night, either. "Of course I'd be willing to have you do that. But I just want you to know I'm not spending the rest of my life searching for some elusive cure that keeps me sicker than I would be without it. I've come through that, and now I just want peace, and the right medicines to keep me from being in too much pain."

She looked up at Sarah and saw the tears in her eyes.

"But the best thing you can do for me right now is to try to help Sarah through this. She hasn't had a lot of experience with cancer. No one in our family has."

She gave Dr. Simpson the name of her doctor and the phone number of his clinic, then called there herself and gave permission for them to release her records. When she turned back to Sarah, she saw that Corinne had left her computer and was sitting on the deck as well. The shock was setting in.

The surf roared against the shore with a voice that was both calming and wearing. Maggie leaned forward, her elbows on her knees. Her short hair stood up in the wind. "I didn't bring you here to get rid of one set of stresses so that you could pick up another one," she said. "I brought you here because I wanted to remind you where you can find rest. In the Bible we're told that there is a Sabbath rest for the people of God. And all through it, we're told not to be anxious, to take our anxieties to the Lord because he cares for us. We're told even by Jesus himself that worrying can't add one moment to anyone's life."

Corinne's hair was a sight, disheveled from bed and the havoc of the wind. "But, Mom, the Bible also says that the Lord helps those who help themselves."

"No, it doesn't," Maggie said. "It doesn't say that anywhere in the Bible."

"But I was sure —"

"It's not in there," Maggie said. "Read it. I dare you to find it."

"But the *concept* is there," Sarah cut in. "God

gives us common sense. He gives us technology. He gives us drugs, doctors —"

"Of course he does," Maggie interrupted. "Girls, if you could have seen me a few months ago, I was willing to do whatever it took to get past this. I wanted it out of my body. And I put up a really good fight. The best fight of my life, in fact."

"But you can't concede defeat yet," Sarah said. "Not while you still have energy. Not while you still have some health."

"Well, see, that's the thing," Maggie said. "I don't really consider it a defeat anymore. When I finally close my eyes and breathe my last breath, I think I'll have won the fight. It won't be a loss."

She might have known that the girls wouldn't take that well, and they both began to weep. She got up, pulled them both against her, and held them for a long time as the ocean wind whispered comforting choruses in their ears.

"I don't want the rest of this week to be filled with gloom and doom," she said. "I really, really don't. The week started out badly, and now it looks like it's taken a turn for the worse. Girls, please, for me, can't you honor your mother and just do a few things I want to do?"

They stepped back, all acquiescence. "Of course we can, Mom," Sarah said. "What do you want to do?"

"I want to see that phone put up where I can't hear it ring and nobody will be walking around with it growing out of their ear," she said. "And I want that computer packed away. And I want to go shopping. I want to look at antiques. I want to go out to eat. I want to see a movie. Or I want to rent a boat and go sailing. There's a little island off the coast everybody talks about. I want to go out there and just lie on the sand and read."

"I don't think we can do all that in one day," Corinne said.

"Then let's just cram as much as we comfortably can into today," Maggie said. She looked at her watch. "I'm starving to death. If you two don't go get ready for breakfast in the next ten minutes, I'm going to have to leave without you."

"Mom, are you sure you're up to this?"

"Yes," she said. "How many times do I have to tell you?" She clapped her hands hard, as she had when they were children. "Now go!"

They both scurried into the house. When the door closed behind them, she leaned her head back on the deck's railing and looked up at the sky. It was blue and there wasn't a cloud. She felt the warmth of God's smile on her face.

"I know it's a tall order, Lord," she said out loud, "but I sure would like to see some joy in these girls before I send them home. Not an easy task when I've just told them I'm dying. But a few minutes of their joy and their peace is all I ask."

Even though there wasn't a word spoken in

reply, she knew that God had registered her request, and that he was already acting on it.

As they shopped and played and ate that afternoon, Maggie snapped four rolls of film, hoping for the perfect shot. When Maggie wasn't snapping pictures, Corinne had the camera in her hands and was snapping shots of her own. Maggie hadn't been photographed so much in her whole adult life. Occasionally, Sarah would take some pictures of Corinne and Maggie, then one of them would ask a stranger to get all three of them.

Maggie had to admit that she hadn't had more fun in years. Her daughters gave her the gift of silliness as they went in and out of antique shops, bought things they didn't need, and tried to guess at items that only the store manager and the craftsman himself could identify.

By the time they got back that night, they were all exhausted. Sarah had rented a movie, *Whatever Happened to Baby Jane*, and they watched it, captivated by the sibling rivalry that had ruined the women's lives. Sarah and Corinne teased each other throughout the movie. Maggie went to bed feeling warm and comforted, and once again slept more deeply than she had in months.

chapter sixteen

The next morning, Corinne and Sarah went with Maggie to the photography studio where she planned to develop the pictures they had taken yesterday. There was hardly room for the three of them, but they squeezed in and watched their mother work.

As the pictures began to come into focus, they saw that some of them were gems. Sarah walked down the row as they hung on the line, studying each one individually.

"Is this one of yours, Corinne?" she asked, pointing to one of her mother and herself.

"Obviously," Corinne said with a giggle, "since you were in the picture."

"Well, it could have been a stranger."

"We only got strangers to take the pictures we were *all* in," Corinne said. She studied the picture. "Yep, that's mine all right."

"You know, you're pretty good," Sarah said. "I mean, compared to me, you're a pro." Sarah pointed to the ones of Corinne and Maggie. They were off-centered, some were slanted, others were blurry because her hands had been shaking. "I take terrible pictures. But look at yours. I think you have talent, like Mom."

100

Maggie abandoned what she was doing and came to study the pictures. "She's right, Corinne," Maggie said. "Look at that. That's perfect. I couldn't have gotten that better myself."

Corinne smiled. "Really?"

Maggie looked at the rest of the pictures hanging up the line. "You have a good eye, Corinne. Look at this one, this expression you captured on Sarah's face. That's priceless. She looked so natural. She's not posing. You caught her in a great moment. I've tried for days to do that."

"And look at this one of Mom," Sarah said. "Mom, you look so young. You look our age."

"Now that *is* brilliant photography," Maggie said. "Seriously, Corinne, I think you've got something here."

Corinne's eyes twinkled. "Thanks, Mom. I really appreciate that. It means a lot to me. You, too, Sarah."

"I think I'll leave all my photographic equipment to you, Corinne," Maggie said.

Corinne's smile faded. She didn't want to talk about inheritances. "If you want," she whispered.

"I do want," Maggie told her. "I was actually thinking of selling it all when I got to the point where I didn't want to use it anymore. But I'm glad I don't have to. You and I, we have some work to do before I hand it all over to you, though. There's a lot I can teach you."

Corinne looked thoughtfully up at the pictures. "Do you think maybe some day I could make a living at this like you've done?"

"Of course you could," Maggie said. "Why not?"

"I don't know. It seems like there's no real way to earn a living at something like this unless you're killing yourself with overwork day and night."

"Well, you know me," Maggie said. "There have been times when I've killed myself day and night. You can work as hard as you want to in any business. And you saw my friend out there. Milton's got people lined up for his portraits. But it's a good business if you have talent, and the right equipment and technique. I think you have the first one, and I can give you the last two."

When they had finished, they gathered up all the pictures. Corinne was thoughtful as they drove back to the cabin.

chapter seventeen

Clouds moved back in around noon, and it started to rain around two. The three women decided to stay in that afternoon and work on the photo albums their mother had hoped to organize. They sat at the kitchen table, putting the history of their family on the pages of the albums in neatly ordered rows. They laughed and talked and remembered. Hours passed before they worked their way up to the current pictures they had taken yesterday and the day before.

"Do you want these in photo albums, Mom, or do you plan to include them in your book?"

Maggie smiled. "There really isn't a book. I thought about doing one, but it was basically an excuse to get you here. The truth is, these pictures are for you. I wanted something for you to remember me by. And to remember each other."

Their fragile spirits seemed to shatter again, and haunted looks returned to both their eyes. Finally Sarah looked up at her sister.

"Corinne, do you think you could find time to come to St. Louis and take pictures of my family?"

Corinne grinned, surprised and flattered. "Well, sure I could take the time, but why would you want me to do it?"

"Well," Sarah said, "it's been a long time since we've had family pictures. And I don't want them to be posed in a studio. First of all, I don't think I could get everybody dressed and get them there at the same time. And second, you just have a flair for catching something in people's faces." She leaned closer, studying the pictures. "I just want to see what you can do with my kids. Besides, I'd love for you to get to know them better, and I'd like for them to get to know you."

Maggie laughed out loud, surprising them both. "That's a great idea, Corinne, and maybe I could come, too, and teach you some of the tricks I've learned. Oh, Corinne, I'm so excited for you. You're going to be a photographer!"

Corinne frowned. "Well, I don't know about that. I mean, I still do have my businesses."

"But this is something you're so good at."

"Hey, I'm good at Web sites and jewelry and walking dogs. Sort of."

"Of course you are," Maggie said, "but this is something different. I've had an amazing life. I've traveled everywhere, photographed everything. And I've had this dream of going around the world one more time and taking pictures of places and people in whose lives God is working. That's one of my regrets, that I didn't get a chance to do that."

"You could do it now, Mom," Corinne said. "It's not too late, is it?"

"Yes, it is," Maggie said. "I really don't have the energy to do it anymore. But maybe you do."

Corinne looked so stricken that Maggie took her hand. "Honey, I hope I'm not putting pressure on you to do something you don't want to do. I mean if you don't want to be a photographer, I certainly don't want you thinking of it as one of my last requests. It's nothing like that. I want you to do what makes you happy. I want you to do what God has planned for you. And I think I know how to help you with that."

Maggie looked from one to the other, then continued. "There's a small inheritance. I managed to save a nest egg over the years. And as I'm sitting here thinking about your future, I'm realizing that I don't want you to have to wait until I'm gone to use it. Corinne, if I gave you your half now, maybe you could slow down and quit worrying so much about making a living. Maybe you could pursue what you love, whether that's photography or something else."

The distress on Corinne's face grew more intense. "Mom, I couldn't take that. You're going to beat this. You'll need the money."

"I'll still have plenty, but I don't think I'm going to need it," she said gently. She turned to Sarah. A vein stood out on her forehead, and she knew she was making a valiant effort not to cry. "Sarah, I want you to use it to take your family on vacation every year. Teach them to walk along the beach, listen to the waves, breathe in the salty air. I want you to teach them that investing in their soul is as important as investing in a business or church, or any number of other things."

Sarah forced herself to nod. "I will, Mom." Then she sighed and looked down at the photos on the table. "I was just looking at this, Mom, at the pictures you took of me the other day, and the ones yesterday and today. And I see all those worry lines and all the anxiety, the tension, the distraction. I see a million things pulling at me, and nothing I do has a very big impact. You know, I'm starting to think that maybe I have a gift, too. A calling, if you will. It's not photography," she said with a chuckle, "but maybe it's deeper than fund raisers and committees and conferences."

"What is it?" Corinne asked.

"Yes, Sarah," Maggie said. "Tell us what it is."

"I'm a mother," Sarah said, lifting her chin high. "And a wife. That's a high calling," she said. "I'm blessed, as my dear little sister pointed out to me the other day. Very blessed. Only I haven't been acting like it."

"So what are you going to do about it?" Maggie asked.

Sarah sat back in her chair and shook her head. "I don't know, Mom. Maybe I need to clear a few things from my day planner."

"Maybe you need to quit *carrying* a day planner," Corinne said.

Sarah laughed and pointed at her as if she had something there. "I think the main thing is that I need to slow down and live deeper. So far I've just been skimming the surface. But I think there's a lot more underneath."

Maggie nodded with glee. "Yes," she said, almost buoyant with pride. "That's exactly what I wanted you to learn. That's exactly it."

When they got back from eating a five-course dinner that night in an expensive candlelit restaurant, they were all full and feeling mellow. The phone was ringing as they came into the cabin, and Maggie answered it.

Sarah could tell from her mother's voice that it was Jim, and as Maggie exchanged words with him, Sarah realized she hadn't thought of calling him in a couple of days. Not since she'd learned of the cancer. It was probably a good thing, she thought, since Jim had been so angry at her the last time they'd spoken. Maybe he'd had time to get over it. She certainly had.

Her mother held the phone out to her. She took it and pulled the cord into the bedroom for some privacy. When she was alone, she put the phone to her ear. "Hello?"

"Hi, babe." She could hear in Jim's endearment that he was no longer mad at her, and she sank onto the bed with relief.

"Hi, honey. Sorry I didn't call yesterday."

"Or the day before," he said. "I was trying to wait you out like we were in high school or something and I didn't want to be the first one to call.

But I started missing you and I couldn't help wondering . . ."

Sarah smiled and closed her eyes in sweet relief. "We just got broadsided with an announcement Mom made," Sarah said, "and it distracted me from everything else."

"What is it?" Jim asked.

The words seemed to stick in her throat. "Mom has cancer."

She listened to his silence as the words sank in. "What kind of cancer? Where is it?"

"Everywhere," she said. "She's had it for some time." She pressed her tear ducts, but the pressure failed to stop her tears. "She's kept it from us, and she's been through some real aggressive chemo and radiation treatments. She claims they've tried everything." Her voice was cracked and high-pitched as she spouted out the words. "The prognosis is not good, Jim."

She heard him slowly exhale. "Are you all right?"

The compassion in his voice moved her, and she shook her head. "No, not really. It's been hard. And I feel so guilty," she said. "There Mom was, asking us to spend one week with her at the end of her life, and what do we do? We act like we have to fit her into our busy schedules. We were making phone calls and doing business, and she kept waiting and waiting . . ."

"Don't do that to yourself," Jim said. "You're there now. You're spending the time. Is she in pain? Does she look sick?"

"No, not really," she said. "I mean, her hair was cut really short and we didn't know why until we realized that it's just growing back in since the chemo. And she's gotten thin. But other than being tired, she seems to be okay right now."

"How's Corinne taking it?"

"Not well," Sarah said. "I called Keith Simpson at home and talked to him."

"Was he able to offer any hope?"

"He's ordered Mom's records from her doctor. He said he would study her file. I know that if there's anything her doctors haven't thought of, he'll come up with it." She covered her mouth and tried to muffle the sob in her throat. "Mom's reconciled herself to death. And the thing is, she's not depressed about it. She seems to be having the time of her life, at least today."

She got quiet for a moment and reached for a towel she had laid on her bedspread. She wiped her face with it, not wanting her mother to know she'd been crying again.

"I'm sorry I gave you another reason to be upset," Jim whispered. "I shouldn't have treated you like that. You've had a lot of pressure, and now it's even worse."

"It's okay, Jim," she said. "I had it coming. But I'm going to change. I promise I am."

"Change how?" Jim asked.

She squeezed her eyes shut and took a deep breath. "I'm going to do less, not more. I'm going to slow down, walk instead of run, order pizza, listen . . ." Her throat tightened. "When I get to the end of my life, I don't think anybody's going to care a whit about all the conferences I directed, or what committees I chaired. But I want to know I did the best things for the people I love. Jim, I'm going to resign from my position as literary chair, and I don't think I'm going to renew my commitment to teach at church when this session is finished. I think I just need a little while to get my head clear, get my focus right, my priorities straight."

"Oh, Sarah," he said. She could almost hear the smile in his voice. "Do you know that I love you?"

She nodded her head, so thankful that he did. "Yes," she whispered, "and do you know that I love you?"

"Yeah," he said. "Somewhere behind all the anxiety, I've known it all along."

"I'm going to need your help," Sarah said.

"I'd rather help you with that than with misspelled programs. And frankly, I like pizza a lot more than chicken casserole."

She laughed then. Relief warmed her all the way to her toes.

chapter eighteen

When Maggie had gone to bed, Corinne and Sarah went out onto the beach again. The air was still tonight, and the moon almost full. Brilliant stars performed in the sky overhead.

"So how are we going to talk her into trying more treatment?" Corinne asked.

Sarah shook her head. "I don't know. We'll cross that bridge when we come to it. First, we've got to wait until Keith Simpson looks over her file. There may not even be any other treatments."

"Of course there are. They can send men to the moon. They can clone animals, for pete's sake. Surely there's something that can be done about Mom's cancer. I mean, look at her. She's young. She's strong."

"She's ready to go," Sarah whispered.

Corinne sat down in the wet sand and lay back, not caring about her hair getting soaked and sandy as the water came up around her. Staring up at the sky, she whispered, "I refuse to believe that. Why would she let go like this? Why would she give up? It's not a weakness to keep fighting."

"Maybe it was such a huge fight that she

couldn't go on. You know, I can't believe she didn't call us and get us to fight it with her."

"She thought she could handle it herself," Corinne said. "That's what we do in our family. We handle things ourselves."

Sarah shook her head. "But I have friends who've gone through cancer treatments. I can't imagine them doing it alone."

"She said she wasn't alone," Corinne said. "She has a support system. She has a whole world we don't know anything about." She saw her sister staring at the sand, her finger idly doodling in it. "Are you going to make another list, Sarah?"

Sarah looked down at the sand as if considering it, then shook her head and dropped flat on her back next to Corinne. As they both gazed up at the stars, she whispered, "No, no list."

Silence lay between them, comforting them as they looked up.

"What do you think heaven's like?" Sarah asked after a while.

Corinne shook her head. "You ask me when I don't even know what is and isn't in the Bible? I can't believe I thought 'the Lord helps those who help themselves' was in there. I've heard it a million times. I know I have."

"Like I said," Sarah said, "the concept is there." She drew in a deep breath and tried to wrack her brain to remember what she knew about heaven. "I remember reading that there are no tears in heaven."

"Sorry," Corinne piped in. "That's an Eric Clapton song."

Sarah chuckled. "No, it really is in the Bible. It says that the Lamb will be their shepherd and guide them to springs of the Water of Life, and that God will wipe every tear from their eyes. It's somewhere in Revelation. I remember because Jenny said it in a play. I had to help her learn her lines. And there's another place, too, at the end of Revelation in chapter 21 or 22. It says, 'He shall wipe away every tear from their eyes and there shall no longer be any death. There shall no longer be any mourning or crying or pain. The first things have passed away.' "

"Sounds like some kind of place," Corinne whispered.

"Maybe that's why Mom wants to go."

"Do you think they eat there?" Corinne asked.

Sarah shot her a puzzled look. "Of course they eat there. Why?"

"Because you ought to be able to eat what you want in heaven."

"Yeah," Sarah said, "that would be great. And I bet they don't have scales."

More silence covered them, as warm and soft as the waves nipping at their toes.

"Do you think we'll recognize people?" Corinne asked. "Will we know Mom when we get there?"

"Of course we will," Sarah said. "We'll know her and she'll know us, and we'll have a reunion to beat all reunions."

Corinne's tears were coming harder now, and Sarah heard the sobbing in her throat. "I don't know how I'm going to stand it," she whispered. "Here I am, all alone. With Mom gone, I'll really be out there by myself."

"You're not by yourself," Sarah whispered. "You have me and my family."

"But that's just it. That's *your* family," Corinne said. "What if I never get married, Sarah? What if I never have kids? What if I have to spend the rest of my life completely detached and alone? Without even a mother or father? It could be such a long time."

"Or it could be a short time," Sarah whispered. "Mom could go on Tuesday, and on Wednesday Jesus could come back. And all that wailing and crying and mourning we did would seem so silly then. We'd just look at him and say, 'If we'd only known it was just a day.' "

"And isn't that what days are to God?" Corinne asked. "A thousand years is like one day?"

"Something like that," Sarah said.

"So really, even if it's fifty years, it's still like a few minutes to him — and to her."

Sarah nodded. "Mom is definitely getting the best part of this deal."

"And here we are trying to talk her out of it." Corinne turned her head and regarded her sister in the darkness. "Do you think we could talk her into taking us with her?"

"I think she plans to," Sarah said. "Just not at the same time."

"We're blessed," Corinne whispered.

"Why do you say that?"

"Because we have a mother who taught us what's important. We have a mother who taught us the truth."

"Boy, we've come a long way in a week, haven't we?" Sarah whispered.

Corinne sat up, wet sand marking her back. "It's getting kind of cool out here. You're shivering."

"Let's not go in yet," Sarah said. "What I'd really like to do is pray for Mom, just you and me, out loud. I know God's listening."

"Good idea," Corinne whispered, and together the girls closed their eyes and began to pray to the Father who cared about their future, as the surf rolled against the shore.

chapter nineteen

Sarah woke before dawn, and a parade of regrets kept her from getting to sleep again. She got up, dressed, and walked around the kitchen, thinking about her mother's disappointment at Sarah's behavior during the early part of the week, the things her mother wanted to do, and how little time she had left.

An idea occurred to her as the sun began to rise. Quickly, she got the car keys and hurried outside. She drove the rental car down the highway that ran along the beach until she came to a pier where dozens of boats sat docked at intervals on the water. Fishermen were readying their boats for a day's work, and Sarah parked the car and headed for the first one.

It was cool, and she crossed her arms and shivered as she came to the deck. "Excuse me," she called.

One of the fishermen looked up and took a cigar out of his mouth. His skin was red from the wind and the sun, and his eyes were creased as though he was used to squinting in the sunlight. "Yeah?" he asked.

"I'm looking for a boat," she said. "One I can rent. Maybe a big sailboat or something, and someone to drive it?"

The man grinned broadly at her choice of words, and looked at the others. They all chuckled. "You might try up there, last boat on the end," he said, gesturing with the cigar. "Ole Jake rents. He'll take you where you want to go."

"Thank you." She hurried up the pier to the boat the man had indicated. She didn't see anyone on board, so she stood there for a moment, wondering if she should step on and call out to him.

"May I help you?"

The voice behind her startled her, and she spun around. "Oh, you scared me."

"Was you lookin' for me?"

She tried to catch her breath. "Uh . . . that depends. Are you Jake?"

"That's me," he said. He was an old man, with tanned skin that looked like cured hide, and deep lines etched into his face. "What can I do for you?"

"I understand you rent your boat out," she said. "My mother and sister and I would like to go out to Fork Island today. Do you rent it by the day?"

"Sure do," he said.

"And you'll . . . uh . . . sail it for us?"

"Yes'm, I will. Cost you three hundred dollars for the day."

She swallowed. "All right. Can we pay you when we get on? I need to go by an ATM."

"Sure," he said. "When you comin'?"

She checked her watch. "Around eight?"

"I'll have 'er ready. You'll like the *Morning Star*. She sails sweet, she does."

Sarah glanced back at the boat and saw its name printed on the side. "The *Morning Star*. That didn't come from the Bible, did it?"

He grinned again, revealing yellowed teeth. "Believer, are you?"

She smiled. "Yes, I am."

"Then you've come to the right place," he said.

Sarah said a prayer on her way back to the cabin, thanking God for sending her a believer with a boat. She could feel God's hand on their family, as the sun made its way up the sky. Her mother was going to be thrilled.

∞

When Maggie got up, both Sarah and Corinne were already in the kitchen. They had cooked breakfast, made coffee, and cleaned up the clutter they had left the night before. Maggie eyed them suspiciously.

"What? No telephones? No computers?"

"No, Mom," Sarah said. "We've got a surprise for you this morning, so go on and get dressed. As soon as we finish breakfast, we're heading out."

"Heading out? Where?"

"You'll see," Corinne said. "Brace yourself. You're going to love it."

They finished breakfast and cleaned the

118

dishes, then headed up the highway. As they drove up to the pier, Maggie's eyes lit up. "A boat," she said. "You didn't!"

"We rented it for the whole day," Corinne said. "Actually, Sarah rented it. She came out here at the crack of dawn this morning and found somebody who could take us out."

"Oh, Sarah!" Maggie cried. "It's just what I wanted. Look at it!" She got out of the car and started up the pier. "It's beautiful."

"It's named the *Morning Star*, Mom," Sarah said, carefully holding back her emotion at her mother's joy. "The owner is a believer."

"The *Morning Star*," Maggie whispered. "From Revelation 22. 'I am the Root and the Offspring of David, and the bright Morning Star.' It's as if God sent it to us. With his stamp of approval."

Already, Maggie had her camera to her eye and was snapping memorials to this special day.

Sarah didn't think she had ever had a moment of greater peace than she did that morning as the boat sailed across the waves, the breeze tossed her hair, and the sun shone down on her shoulders.

As Old Jake raised the sail and took them out onto the quiet ocean, away from everything loud and fast and anxious, Sarah almost felt as though she didn't have a care in the world. It was as if the troubles of her mother's illness and all that reality meant to Sarah had been left on the shore.

The *Morning Star* had mercifully given her a day's reprieve.

☙

Behind Sarah, Corinne glanced at her mother — asleep on the deck — and wondered whether she had been in any pain this morning. Had she slept last night? But there was no struggle on Maggie's face. No battle fatigue. Only peace.

Corinne leaned over the side, watching the waves for dolphins, looking up for seagulls, or across the water for an occasional shark emerging in the distance. Like a shark, death was circling her family, closing in on their mother, threatening to devour her. But today, Corinne didn't see it as something evil to be avoided. Today she saw it as an end to a full life, a transition into something even greater. And that simple fact amazed her. Such a thought could not have come from her own frightened heart. It was a supernatural understanding, a gift from their Great Counselor.

A tear rolled down her face, and she wiped it away. *I wish I could experience that rest Mom talked about,* she told the Lord. *Help me to find that rest.* She looked at her sleeping mother and realized this woman she had known all her life had found the source of true rest, and her spirit was healthy and whole, even while the cancer ravaged her body.

"It'll be all right, Mom," Corinne whispered, knowing no one could hear. "It will be all right."

And as the boat sailed serenely across the sea, she knew that, somehow, God would make it so.

Later, when Maggie was awake and they had almost reached the island, the old sailor offered to take their picture. They squeezed in together, the waves and the sky at their back. He snapped the picture without much attention to focusing or zooming, or positioning them in the frame. He just snapped the shutter and handed the camera back.

It was almost dark when they got back to the mainland, sunburned and sandy but tranquil and tired. Maggie was anxious to get the film developed. She insisted on going to the studio alone, because she wanted to surprise them if anything good came of the pictures, so Sarah and Corinne busied themselves around the cabin, cooking supper and waiting for her to return, basking in the peace they had brought back with them.

chapter twenty

Maggie wept that night as she stood over the developing trays. Clearly, the picture the old sailor had taken of them was the best one. If there had really been a book of memories of her life, this would have been on the cover.

She could see the evidence of the cancer in her face. There were lines around her eyes and her mouth, and a gaunt hollowness in her cheeks. But she could also see the peace and great joy in her eyes. And miraculously, she could see it in Corinne's and Sarah's sunburned faces, too. It was an answer to prayer.

The lines around their eyes had vanished, and they looked young again, untarnished by the world and its problems. They were smiling genuine smiles, though no one had told them to say cheese. Their eyes were relaxed. Their faces were at rest. Wind blew their hair from side to side, and the sea had sprayed a fine mist over their faces, but they both looked more beautiful than she had ever seen them.

This was the one. This was what she had come for.

She went out and got Milton. After he had admired the print, he helped her blow it up and copy it so that each of the girls could take a print home, and remember this day for the rest of their lives.

As she started to leave the studio, her friend stopped her at the door. "I'm glad you had a good day, Mags."

She laughed softly. "I've accomplished everything I came here for. I think my work is done."

"Good," he whispered. "That's real good, Mags."

"We're going home tomorrow. Corinne has to get back to her businesses, and Sarah has to get back to her family. Seven days. That's all we had. But it was a good seven days."

"I'm going to miss you," he whispered, looking at her with the familiar eyes of a friend who knew this was a final good-bye.

"I'll miss you, too," she whispered, "but I'll see you again someday. Someday real soon." She reached up and hugged him tightly, and as she drove away from that place, she looked in her rearview mirror. It was okay, she thought. He was a brother of hers under God, and if it was their final earthly good-bye, their reunion would be a grand one.

chapter twenty-one

Corinne and Sarah awoke teary-eyed the next morning, and were quiet as they packed to go home. Maggie moved around the cabin, trying to help as much as she could. She wished now she had booked them on afternoon flights, but the midmorning ones had seemed like a better idea at the time.

As they drove to the airport, she heard occasional sniffing in the backseat. Glancing in the rearview mirror, she saw Corinne wiping her face. In the passenger seat, Sarah stared out her window as if to hide her face from her mother.

"This isn't the last time we're going to see each other, you know," Maggie said softly. "I plan to come visit. And you'll come to see me, won't you?"

Sarah's chin came up. "You know I will, don't you? I mean, I haven't been a very good daughter to this point, but I'm not going to let you go through the rest of this alone."

"Neither am I," Corinne said, leaning forward. "And you've got to teach me all you know about photography, show me how to use the equipment, everything. I plan to visit you in a week or so."

"You're both welcome to come anytime, but you have your own lives, and I don't want to be a burden to you."

"You're not a burden, Mom," Sarah said, as though disgusted at the thought. "If this week has taught me anything, it's that the world won't fall apart if I'm not at home. The kids go on. Jim does a good job taking care of them. I want to come and be with you." She swallowed hard, trying to steady her voice. "Mom, I want to give you your medicine. I want to bring you water in bed at night. I want to drive you to the doctor."

Maggie had vowed not to cry, but she knew she couldn't keep that vow.

"I want to get you well," Sarah said. "And if that doesn't happen . . . well, I want to know I did my very best."

"Honey, if your best gets any better, I'll be too puffed up with pride to get through those pearly gates. You just be yourself, Sarah. You're doing fine." She reached behind her for Corinne's hand. "You, too, honey."

They were quiet the rest of the way to the airport. After they checked Sarah's baggage, they hurried to Corinne's gate, since hers was the first flight out.

"Now as soon as you get things in order, you call me and we'll work out your coming to see me," Maggie said. "I'll get you started on that new career."

"That'll be good, Mom," Corinne whispered. She looked at her mother for a moment, then hugged her as tightly as if it was the last time.

Sarah stepped up, too, and held them both. "I don't know if I have the strength to let you go," she whispered.

"God will help you," Maggie said. "He's just waiting to be asked."

chapter twenty-two

Several hours later, Corinne walked into her apartment, where her personal three-ring circus was usually in progress. The answering machine light was blinking, calling her attention to all the calls she had to return. She turned on her computer and checked her e-mail, and began counting the problems. One was from V-Tech, whose Web site hadn't been working. She hadn't even called her contact there for the last three days, not since she'd learned of her mother's cancer. She supposed he was livid, and she couldn't blame him.

She sat down wearily and dialed the client's number. "May I speak to Mr. Black, please? This is Corinne Downing, of Downing Enterprises."

The secretary hesitated. "Uh . . . He doesn't want to speak to you, Corinne."

She closed her eyes. "He doesn't want to speak to me? Why not?"

"He said for me to tell you that he won't be needing your services anymore. They've hired another Web designer."

She leaned back hard in her chair, her mind racing for ways to talk him out of it. Maybe it was worth a shot. Maybe if she could get over there right now, meet with him face to face, explain about her mother's cancer. If she could make him understand why she had dropped the ball, maybe he would reconsider. But even as the thought occurred to her, she quickly discarded it. She didn't want to do this anymore.

"Well, thank you very much," she said to the secretary. "It's been nice working with you. Please tell Mr. Black that I hope everything goes well with his new designer."

Corinne hung up the phone, and a soft smile crept across her face. It was okay. If she'd lost this client a week ago, she'd have panicked. But today she took it in stride. It was time to cut some ties. Time to simplify. Time to focus on the important things. And her mother's gift would help with that.

She called her friend who had been managing her dog-walking business for the last week.

"Anne Grayter here," she answered, sounding frazzled.

"Hi, Anne. It's Corinne. So, how's it going?"

"Corinne, you're back?" She sounded disappointed. "It's going great. I picked up three new clients for you."

"Three new clients? Anne, I can only handle the ones I have."

"Well, maybe I could help," she said. "I really love this. It's a great gig."

Corinne's eyes twinkled as she thought it over for a second. Then she blurted out, "How would you like to buy the business?"

"I'd love it. Are you kidding? This is perfect for me!"

"Come on over later today," Corinne said, "and we'll talk about it."

"Do you want me to keep doing it today until we do?"

"If you don't mind," Corinne said. "I don't really have the energy."

"I'll be there around five," her friend said.

Corinne hung up, laughing softly at the way she'd just so easily shaken off two of her biggest moneymakers — and her two biggest headaches. What would she do now? Photography, she thought. She would become a photographer like her mother. She would pour her energy and her time into something she was drawn to, something she was good at, and she would quit spreading herself so thin that she couldn't be good at anything.

She got online, went to a cyberspace bookstore, and shopped for books on photography. When she clicked the cash register icon to check out, she smiled at how easily it worked. Why hadn't V-Tech's site worked this well? She shook her head, thankful that it was no longer her problem.

Meanwhile, she would concentrate on her relationships, and she would start by visiting Sarah and photographing her husband and kids.

chapter twenty-three

Jim was waiting at the airport when Sarah got off the plane, and before the kids could attack her, he pulled her into his arms and held her with a crushing embrace. She melted with gratitude.

"I'm so sorry about your mom," he whispered, kissing her hair. "I'm so sorry that you had to go through that alone."

"Oh, I wasn't alone," she whispered, "not by a long shot."

He pulled back and wiped her eyes, kissed her cheek, then stepped back and allowed her children to throw their arms around her, as if she'd been gone for a year instead of just a few days.

She hugged them tight, laughing with delight as they chattered nonstop about all the things they'd done while she was gone. And even though it sounded like they'd had a laugh a minute, she could tell that they had missed her and were glad to have her home.

As they got her bag and headed out to the car, her son looked up at her. "Hey, Mom, what's for supper?"

Sarah thought it over for a moment, then a grin tiptoed across her face.

"Supper?" she repeated. "I think we'll have pie."

Jenny's eyes grew wide. "No way."

Chase gaped up at her, stunned, and Jim started to laugh. "That's my girl," he said.

chapter twenty-four

Maggie drove back to the cabin after she'd taken the girls to the airport. She climbed into bed and napped with the earnestness of a newborn.

It was time for the sun to set when she awoke, so she went out onto the deck, found a comfortable chair, and watched that gold burst of fire melting into the water. On the horizon, she saw a sailboat again, moving slowly across the foamy waves.

She wondered if it was the *Morning Star*.

She kept her eyes on it as it made its slow way farther out to sea, growing smaller and smaller in the distance, until she could see it no more. But she knew it was still there. She propped her feet on another chair and leaned her head back against her own. She could sleep for a week. A month, maybe. An eternity. She was that tired. But it was a good kind of tired, one that rested easily in her soul.

The sun made its final burst over the water, its colors spreading out soft and thin on the wispy clouds. She thought of getting her camera, photographing it, selling it as one of her final prints. Beauty to bucks.

But this was just between God and her. She

didn't want to share it.

It was her silent farewell, her joyful hello . . . his sweet comfort, her grateful acceptance . . .

. . . before her boat sailed for brighter skies.

CB 3/03

mG 7/0v

NE
2/02

ML